AF242079

Wyoming Destiny: Hope Triumphs Over Fate

Also by Mark Greathouse

The Wolf's Tales

The Wolf's Quest: Isa's Adventure Begins

The Frontier Calls: Two Spirits, One Adventure

Wild Horses on the Laramie: A Life of No Boundaries

The Frontier Chronicles

Perilous Trails: Jack's Adventure Begins

Wyoming Calls: Jack's Risky Quest

Longhorns North: Jack's Great Trail Drive

Warpath: Jack's Faith is Tested

Hunter Vs. Hunted: Jack's Great Frontier Challenge

Freedom Drovers: Jack's Awesome Crusade

A Poison Spreads: Jack Seeks the Antidote

Darkness Looms: Jack Faces War

The Tumbleweed Sagas

Nueces Justice

Nueces Reprise

Nueces Deceit

Nueces Blood

Nueces Grit

Nueces Truth

Nueces Legend

The Tumbleweed Sagas - Junior's Story

Lone Star Vigilante

Guns on the Guadalupe

Railroad to Perdition

The Black Gold Mob

Pale Horse of the Apocalypse

Nicholas Dunn: The Making of a Texas Legend (A Western Adventure)

Wyoming Destiny: Hope Triumphs Over Fate

The Wolf's Tales

Book Four

Mark Greathouse

Wyoming Destiny: Hope Triumphs Over Fate
Paperback Edition
Copyright © 2026 by Mark Greathouse

WISE WOLF BOOKS
An Imprint of Wolfpack Publishing
1707 E. Diana Street
Tampa, FL 33610

wisewolfbooks.com

All rights reserved. No part of this book may be reproduced in any form or by any electronic or mechanical means, including information storage and retrieval systems, without express written permission from the publisher, except for the use of brief quotations in reviews. Any use of this publication to train generative artificial intelligence (AI) technologies is expressly prohibited.

This book is a work of fiction. References to historical events, real people, or real places are used fictitiously. Any similarity to real persons, living or dead, is purely coincidental and not intended by the author.

Paperback ISBN 978-1-968733-81-0
eBook ISBN 978-1-968733-80-3

Dedicated with love to my wife Carolyn and our two sons, Mike and Matt.

Don't be deceived: God is not mocked. For whatever a man sows he will also reap.

    —Galatians 6:7

But you are a chosen race, a royal priesthood, a holy nation, a people for His possession, so that you may proclaim the praises of the One who called you out of darkness into His marvelous light.

    —1 Peter 2:9

Be serious! Be alert! Your adversary the Devil is prowling around like a roaring lion, looking for anyone he can devour.

    —1 Peter 5:8

The Cast

The Cast

Isa (aka, Wolf) O'Toole—*Twenty-two-year-old son of Jack O'Toole, whose quest is to venture alone into the great frontier of the North Platte River country. Isa translates to wolf in the Comanche tongue.*

Awentia (aka, Morning Star)—*Twenty-one-year-old daughter of Lakota warrior Wapitiyu Okle (Spotted Elk) and granddaughter to Chief Lone Horn. She's married to Isa. They have sons named Moses and Michael.*

Jack O'Toole—*Father to Isa. Earned Comanche name Pohya Isa, Walks With Wolves.*

Blue Flower—*Young sister to Spirit Talker and daughter to Buffalo Hump, she's married to Jack. They have three children: Isa, Peter, and Nadua.*

George Freeman—*A Black cowboy who establishes the Circled Cross Ranch on the North Platte River in Wyoming. Father to Esmeralda. Adopts Lakota child, Zebediah.*

Running Waters—*George Freeman's Pawnee wife.*

Esmeralda Freeman—*George's and Running Waters' fourteen-year-old daughter.*

Zebediah Freeman—*Foundling, Lakota son to George and Running Waters.*

Taabe—*Wolf offspring of Zebediah.*

Wapitiyu Okle (aka, Spotted Elk)—*Miniconjou Lakota that is Morning Star's father.*

Will "Wally" Wallace—*Elderly mountain man who roamed the wilds of the frontier.*

Hap Cole and Dred Evans—*Cowboys on George Freeman's ranch.*

Chester Donovan—*First hand hired on the Laramie Cross Breed Ranch.*

Connor Culthwaite—*Ranching neighbor to Isa and Awentia.*

Will Cutter and Joe Moon—*Wranglers hired to work the Laramie Cross Breed Ranch.*

John Granger—*Itinerate cowpoke looking to travel to Oregon but prejudiced toward Indians.*

HISTORICAL CHARACTERS

Tatanka Iyotake (aka, Sitting Bull)—*Hunkpapa Lakota holy man and chief who inspired plains tribes to fight the White settlers. His warriors help defeat General Custer at Little Bighorn.*

General George Crook—*Based out of Fort Laramie in 1876, his assignment was to eradicate the "Indian Problem." He then headed the Department of the Platte with headquarters at Fort Omaha in North Omaha, Nebraska.*

Charles Arthur Guernsey—*A legislator, rancher, and mining promoter from Cooperstown, New York, who arrived at The Emigrant's Washtub in 1880 and for whom the town of Guernsey was eventually named.*

August Klappenbach—*Co-founder and early enterprising resident of Bandera, Texas.*

Captain Edward Hayes—*Commandant of Fort Laramie in 1881.*

Hubert and Arthur Teschemacher—*Wealthy brothers who founded the Cheyenne Club and led the Wyoming Stock Growers Association.*

Charles Goodnight—*Former Texas Ranger who cofounded the JA Ranch in Palo Duro Canyon with John Adair.*

James McLaughlin—*Indian Agent for the Standing Rock Agency at Fort Yates, ND.*

Wyoming Destiny: Hope Triumphs Over Fate

You are invited

Dear Reader,

A young half-breed, a one-man pony, a warrior woman, and a wolf tame the American frontier. That about sums my story. If you're reading the Wolf Tales series, then it's likely that *Perilous Trails* and my pa's Frontier Chronicles series must have fully grabbed you. This fourth part of my tale begins in 1881, a few years after I left home on a vision quest. I am twenty-two years old and very much a grown man by frontier standards.

I sure don't recommend dealing with the sort of situation that I left y'all with. That bear was a nasty critter with his ears pinned back and claws out. He was in quite a lather. Obviously, I survived, and therein begins this part of my tale.

Wyoming Destiny: Hope Triumphs Over Fate continues the testing of my courage, faith, endurance, pure grit, and search for a life mission that I share with my warrior woman wife, Morning Star. My folks named me Isa, which translates in Comanche to Wolf. I expect that I should add that my pa is White and my ma is a Comanche. That makes me, my brother Peter, and my young sister Nadua what folks called half-breeds. As you'll find out, this can be a blessing and a heavy burden. Do keep in mind that my story incorporates history not found in most school history books. This book relates my tale as driven by fate and guided by God.

I have met up with plenty of Indians, especially Comanche and Lakota Sioux, so you'll find me using some of their language throughout *Wyoming Destiny: Hope Triumphs Over Fate.* I have provided a handy glossary of Comanche and Lakota words toward the back of this book. I also provide a convenient glossary of frontier terms.

I'm a Christian, but I have tried to grasp the Comanche and Lakota cultures to better understand them. The Indian religion is based upon what is referred to as animism, in which every common natural item—from fish and animals to plants, trees, waterways, and mountains—was believed to have souls or spirits. The spirits and traditions connected with them guided the Comanche and Lakota. Their passion for their spirits no doubt gave them their fearlessness, as fed by the belief that they were protected in everything they did. Would they kill to defend their beliefs? Theirs was not a religion of love and forgiveness.

Could Indians like the Comanche or Lakota become Christians? My stories in the Wolf's Tales share my personal evolution at the intersection of faith and culture.

As you follow my adventures, ask yourself whether you might be up to meeting the challenges I take on. Dangers? Privations? Hmmm. How might you have fared? Through it all, I first relied on the teachings from my family, then went on to learn from the raw and risky experiences I faced. I learned to trust in instincts forged from my biblical lessons.

To be straight here, I had no idea that my story was going to fill multiple volumes until I began to write it all down. I invite you to follow my adventures on America's western frontier.

Kindest regards,
    Isa "Wolf" O'Toole

PROLOGUE

I'd bested the bushwhackers and reckoned to get on with my journey home. The two had been a disappointment, as I'd tried to give them another chance at life. They had designs on stealing my horses and poke, and I'd have none of that. I forgave their ill will and sent them northward to seek their fortunes in the mining country around Deadwood. Seems they never made it. They'd turned on me instead. My shoulder still hurt from the gunshot wound, but I was okay otherwise. I hoped and prayed that it wouldn't get infected. The bullet had gone clean through without hitting bone. I applied some alder bark mixed with peyote as a poultice and bandaged it as best I could. I reckoned that so long as I was careful, I'd make it home without bleeding to death. I thanked God it hadn't been worse. I even asked His forgiveness for what led to my attackers losing their lives. Their deed had been as senseless as their deaths.

As I was about to mount Mukue, I heard the sound no man wants to hear in the forest or anywhere. Mukue's ears shot up, and Taabe raised his hackles and growled. Too late! I turned and found myself looking up at a huge grizzly, standing nine feet tall and not ten feet away.

I uttered a pointless warning. "Don't do it, bear!"

Angry eyes and slobbering fangs gave full voice as to his intentions. He'd appeared as though from nowhere, not even alerting Mukue or Taabe until he was nearly upon us. I didn't hesitate but drew my Colt and fired at point-blank range again and again while yanking my Bowie knife from its sheath. "Lord help me!" I found myself shouting. I know some of my bullets must have hit the grizzly, but the beast charged full bore. In but a heartbeat, I was pressed face to chest with a huge furry mass of pure, hot-breathed fury. "Please, dear God!" came my muffled voice, as I sought air to breathe and space for my Bowie knife. Three-inch claws slashed the air as I strove to swipe inward and upward with my knife.

Chapter 1

Fight For My Life!

I was held tightly in the bear's grasp and fighting for my life. Smothered in fur, blood, and slobber mixed with hot breath and angry growls, all my might was focused on shoving the Bowie knife deep into the bear's belly and cutting upward. I strove desperately to breathe. I was trapped in a bear hug that was a blessing and a curse; blessed because the bear's claws weren't as effective close in, and cursed because using my knife was extremely difficult. I heard Taabe's growls as he buried his fangs in the bear's haunches. The bear fought on pure instinct and couldn't know that he was in a losing battle. I feared that he'd take me with him in death. I buried my knife to the hilt and pulled upward with all the might I could muster. I felt it strike bone and used every ounce of my strength to cut through.

There I was, literally in a bear hug, desperately clinging to the beast by a handful of fur with one hand to avoid those three-inch razor-sharp claws while fervently working my knife into his gut. One of us was going to die. Lord, I prayed it would be him.

My knife cut ever deeper. I could feel his bloody hot entrails against my own chest, yet the beast fought on angrier than ever. What possessed him? "Dear God, make him die!" I cried in desperation.

Seconds passed like hours. I felt the bear's attack begin to weaken. Would I yet survive? Visions of Morning Star flew through my consciousness. My bullets and Bowie knife, coupled with Taabe's powerful jaws, were finally having their effect. Would I outlast the grizzly? Could I? I was beginning to feel the pain from the wounds his claws had managed to deliver into my exposed flesh. I was bleeding; perhaps, more than I realized. The bullet wound in my shoulder from the earlier bushwhacking had surely been torn open.

I felt the bear begin to stagger; his heaviness began to slump against me. The big beast was finally giving out. As I sensed that he was beginning to fall, it took all my effort to avoid him collapsing on top of me. Six or seven hundred pounds of dead bear spread on top of me would not have been a desirable outcome, especially in my deteriorating condition. He at last fell. Thankfully, he fell backward, landing with a resounding thud in the Colorado dust and swiping his paws helplessly a couple of times at thin air.

My battered and bloodied body wound up seated just inches from the bear. The monstrous beast mustered a final angry look at me and reached out with a final weak swipe of a massive paw before he breathed his last. I sat stunned for a couple of moments, then stood up and took stock of myself. I was covered head to toe in blood. On my front was the bear's blood mixed with pieces of entrails, but I could feel my own blood oozing from my back. For whatever reason, my thoughts roamed to fifty years earlier, when it was said that the mountain man

Hugh Glass had been horribly mauled by a grizzly and left for dead, but survived. I lost that thinking in a hurry. This was here and now, and I was very much alive. And, I was Isa O'Toole, not Hugh Glass. I was determined to live!

The bear was a mess. Taabe had torn a great chunk of meat from his haunches, and I'd gutted him. It had taken a few minutes, but the bullets had finally done their job. I counted four bullet holes in the center of the bear's chest. Nevertheless, it was surely by God's grace that I had survived. Taabe stared at me, and I stared back. "What are you looking at?" I asked. My wolf companion seemed to accept that I'd survived, gave a wolfish shrug, and began gnawing at his bear meat prize.

I was helpless to deal with the claw cuts that sliced across my back and shoulders. Bless Taabe, but his paws didn't lend themselves to applying poultices and bandages. Mukue and Bertrum were no better. My only recourse would be to don a fresh buckskin shirt, fasten it tightly to exert pressure, and then pray the bleeding would stop on its own. I stood up, steadied myself, and walked easy-like over to Mukue. He was skittish, as I smelled of bear blood and saliva. I steadied him enough to reach my hand inside my saddlebag. Being the experienced frontiersman that I was and with a strong Comanche heritage, I had a few more of the makings of medicinal poultices in my saddlebags. Praise God that I hadn't used them up to treat my bullet wound.

I proceeded to line my fresh buckskin shirt with as much alder bark and peyote as I could scrape together while having a bit of a chat with God about pain and the poultices fending off infection. I tore a few pieces of fringe from my shredded buckskin shirt to tie the poultices in place as best I could.

It became apparent that my wounds weren't immediately life-threatening, at least judging by my not growing weak from loss of blood. However, infection could yet cause trouble.

I found myself steady enough on my feet that I was able to fetch the two horses that survived my bushwhackers. I'd have them, my pack mule Bertrum, and my spirited mustang stallion Mukue to contend with.

Now, I had a huge dead bear sprawled out before me. Could I just let the beast lie there for scavengers to dispose of? No. Despite my wounds, it wasn't every day that a human killed a grizzly in hand-to-claw combat. I was determined to fight through my pain and skin the grizzly. And, I was beginning to feel some pain. I fetched the skinning knife from my saddlebags, though that was made difficult by Mukue once again being a bit skittish at the scent of bear blood and saliva still covering me.

About this time, I heard a distressed, almost anguished whimpering from upwind of us. The grizzly had a mate. How close was she? What might she do? Were there cubs? I shuddered to imagine another battle with a bear.

With a resigned sigh, I drew my Spencer carbine from its saddle scabbard, checked the load, and leaned it alongside the dead bear. I wasn't going to let a mourning grizzly sow deprive me of the spoils of my fight to the death. As I worked to skin the beast, I kept a watchful eye out for that sow. I felt sorry for her being widowed, but her mate had picked the fight and suffered the consequences. It could have been me bled out on Colorado soil. Eventually, the sow's cries gave out. She ambled off. She'd likely check out her mate's remains after I was long gone. She'd surely survive and find a new mate.

By this time, I realized that I was expending a lot of energy trying to skin six hundred or so pounds of grizzly. I'd partly field dressed him with my Bowie knife during the fight, but that was no concern. Skinning him was likely an idiotic thing to do, as I'd need all the strength I could muster for the trail ahead. To say the least, given my condition and the weight of the bear, my skinning task was shabby. I simply had not the strength to adequately deal with the bear's dead weight.

I'd guess that it took better than an hour—allowing for frequent rests—to finally manage to collect the bear's claws and bundle the heavy head and skin for transport. Dang, but it was heavy. Somehow, I managed to lift it onto Bertrum's back. He wasn't exactly pleased at first to have the remains of a bear lashed across his back, but he got over it.

Praise the Lord, but my legs were in good shape. The bear had spared them. I easily mounted Mukue and began leading my tiny caravan toward Fort Laramie. However, the effect of my cuts and bruises only truly began to concern me after I'd been riding for a couple of hours. The pain wasn't enough to cause me to pass out, but I remained fearful of infection despite the poultices. There was no telling what filth lingered on the bear's claws.

* * *

Desperate to reach Fort Laramie and have my wounds treated by the fort doctor, I pushed Mukue and my entourage at as fast a pace as I could endure. Lingering nearly constantly in my thoughts was holding Morning Star and our children in my arms. I'd reach the fort in four days, so long as I didn't linger. I feared stopping, as my aching muscles already fought off cramping and stiffness. Mukue's rocking motion helped keep my leg muscles limber, but didn't do much for my upper body.

The occasional rocky landscape and loose soil, coupled with giving the horses respite by dismounting now and then, did conspire to slow my travels. On top of it all, I remained vigilant for any hostiles, as Arapaho, Cheyenne, and even Lakota were still known to haunt these hills. There were also rumors of the return of Sitting Bull. Through it all, my wounds and bruises became ever more painful. One cut from the bear's claws ran from my shoulder to my elbow, down the back of my arm. It was causing me considerable concern, as my lower arm and hand were beginning to go numb and discolor. If physical trials did indeed build strength, I reckoned I'd come out of this a very powerful man—at least so far as my faith in God. He didn't always provide the most ideal life conditions, and He had surely delivered a major test this day.

* * *

I journeyed doggedly toward Fort Laramie, even deciding to ride straight through the first night. The decision was driven by the ongoing fear that my muscles would tighten from the battering they'd absorbed, and I'd be unable to mount Mukue. Shucks, if I laid down, I worried that I might not be able to get up.

Come morning of the next day, I saw a pair of vultures circle lazily overhead on thermal currents. They were appropriately ugly birds well suited to scavenging. I prayed they weren't waiting for me.

I finally decided to risk stopping, so for the second night, I made a cold camp to catch some sleep after having traveled a seemingly interminable distance. It was all I could do to make a campsite and then stagger from horse to horse to mule to be sure all were well. I yearned for a warm fire and hot coffee, but was in poor condition for defending myself and feared that hostiles might be around. I dared not alert them. I chewed on bits of raw bear meat and drank water from a nearby creek to keep up my strength as best I could.

I had scant poultice makings remaining, but nevertheless did my level best to shed the old medicines from my wounds and line my shirt with the last of the alder bark and peyote. I hoped these would fend off infection until we reached the fort.

Next morning, I fought off the stiffness and pain to mount Mukue. In my ever-weakening condition, I had scant appreciation for the changes in the landscape. Texas, the land of my birth and heritage, held my heart, but Wyoming held a pure, undiluted beauty that I'd fallen in love with. God had outdone Himself, as distant mountains and rushing streams offered their siren call. Was this my destiny? Hope lay ahead. I kept telling myself that I'd make it to Fort Laramie.

The rhythm of the horse's hooves and swaying of his pace actually brought me a little tranquility, though I found myself occasionally pounding my legs with my fists to stay alert for danger. I nearly fell from my saddle a couple of times during the second day and gave thought to tying myself to it. I tossed off that idea, as I hadn't the strength.

I fell asleep in the saddle a time or two as lulled by the rhythm of the ride but was awakened by jostling, as Mukue would step to avoid occasional obstacles. I was grateful that he was sure-footed. He seemed to understand my condition and was as gentle as possible given the rough terrain.

Toward sundown of the third day, as the first shadows stretched away from the forested mountain slopes to the west, I yielded once again to my desperate need for rest. I could bear the saddle no longer without relief.

As darkness descended this night amid the flitter of bats, chirp of crickets, and distant hooting of owls and coyote howls, I lay my body out in the midst of the prairie grasses and fell into a pain-induced sleep. My pa once told me that the trail we travel leaves evidence of the character of the man following it, even his very soul. That I'd endured this far despite my wounds likely embodied that very ideal and more. I was driven by faith-grounded hope and my drive to hold Morning Star and my sons close to me again. The mountain man Hugh Glass had been far worse off than me yet traveled more than two hundred miles on foot to safety. My journey was merely two-thirds as far, and I was blessed with a horse.

I awakened to Taabe's cold nose nuzzling my cheek. Shards of sunlight shot through the nearby lodgepole pine. A small herd of elk sauntered past where I lay. Life surrounded me. I refused to even consider dying. I'd make it to Fort Laramie.

I felt my wounds tear a bit as I struggled to stand. With my supply of poultices depleted, I could do nothing more about them other than pray they wouldn't become infected. Perhaps, they already were. My left arm especially worried me. Mukue stood close by patiently awaiting my attempt to mount him. Even Bertrum showed his appreciation by offering a low whinny and prancing in place as though anxious to resume our journey.

Mounting Mukue was no easy task. Every muscle in my body was stiff and ached terribly. My bruised bones had begun to scream silently at a mere touch. I took his reins in my right hand—my left arm was growing useless—and limped to a fallen log. I positioned Mukue beside the log and managed to climb onto it and slide onto the saddle. Oh, but it hurt. I'm afraid I took the Lord's name in vain a couple of times. My pa had told me that life was like a story and each event we encountered added chapters. God had a reason for each. Whatever His reason, he was adding a highly challenging chapter this day. However, I endured and soon had my little caravan reassembled.

We had crossed into Wyoming better than two days ago, and my hopes went sky high when we came upon the Laramie River. By my reckoning, we were now little more than a day from the fort. With hope kindled anew, I became more determined than ever. Despite yearning to immerse myself in the cool, soothing river waters, I pressed on. Simply following the river would take me to the fort.

My left arm was looking terrible. There was now no doubt that infection had settled into my shoulder and upper arm wounds. I reckoned they were downright ugly to see. It dawned on me that I might lose my arm.

Chapter 2

Fort Laramie

Despite my wounds or perhaps because of them, I had ridden better than a hundred and fifty miles in slightly better than four days. The landscape had surely been beautiful, but I was in no condition to care. I felt fortunate to have not encountered another bear or a mountain lion. My body ached to my very core. Mukue and the rest of my makeshift procession were travel-weary but up to the final push. I felt relief as I wended my way among the tents and teepees pitched around the outskirts of the fort. The gawks of men and women and the laughter of children changed to expressions of awe as my little column limped by. I ignored them. I had to, as my goal finally lay within reach.

I was wretched-looking. Covered in dried blood and trail dust and sweating from the afternoon heat, I did not present a pretty picture. The rolled-up bearskin tied to Bertrum told much of my story and surely caused folks to wonder at the grim visage that rode past them. A little boy formed his hands into claws, bared his teeth, and growled as he pretended to be a bear.

I must have been a sight to the sentry at the fort entrance as I reined in. I barely managed to speak. "I'm Isa O'Toole...I need a..." Everything became lost in a murky haze. I apparently lost consciousness and fell from my saddle in a filthy, bleeding heap.

* * *

I awakened in the dim light of the Fort Laramie medical dispensary. Managing to open my eyes, I became aware that I was lying half-naked on a table. I vaguely overheard what appeared through my blurry vision to be the doctor, a gruff old officer who'd likely served in the War Between the States and in some Indian campaigns.

"Don't know as I can save that arm, Captain," he whispered to the officer standing beside him. "Being a breed, I don't know that it matters except he won't be shooting any bow and arrows." He had the audacity to discount my humanity.

The officer eased over beside me and saw that I'd awakened. "I'm Captain Edward Hayes, the post commandant, O'Toole."

"Don't...don't be taking my arm," I pleaded, my voice a mere shadow.

"Surgeon here says you've got a bad infection, son. It could kill you," he advised.

I sensed he'd seen his share of battlefield hospitals with amputated limbs stacked outside. "You believe in God, Captain?" I asked, desperately determined to save my arm.

"Out here, we all come to believing in the Lord," he replied. He gave a guarded shake of his head to the doctor.

The captain didn't seem especially encouraging. My

head was clearing a bit as I beseeched him. "Well, the good Lord got me here, Captain. If it's His will, I figure to go home to my wife as a whole man." I spoke as firmly as I could muster, fighting off the urge to faint.

"He won't make it, Captain," insisted the surgeon.

Captain Hayes gave me an appraising once-over. "Are you the man who scouted for Stanley and Custer a few years back on the Yellowstone?"

I managed a nod.

"Then you must be the same man who saved the life of then Lieutenant Dickerson," he said as though vividly recalling the incident. The captain turned smartly to the surgeon. "Give this man the best care the 7th US Infantry can offer, Major. And don't you dare amputate that arm."

"God bless you, Captain," I responded.

The surgeon looked askance. He clearly couldn't care less about anyone with Indian blood running in their veins, but he'd follow orders. It was how he'd survived the Army as long as he had. "Yes, sir," he replied unconvincingly but dutifully.

Captain Hayes turned to leave.

"My horse, Captain?"

He smiled. "No one could get near him, son. He did follow that pack mule of yours into the stable. The wolf that was with you ran off. When you're up to talking, I'm interested in learning about those two horses you towed in. Meanwhile, you concentrate on healing." He gave a second look at the surgeon and then back at me. "God will save your arm, son. Don't be fretting," he said confidently and started for the door. He stopped and glanced back. "I especially want to hear about the bear." He smiled and began to head out.

"Thanks, Captain," I managed weakly, as he'd nearly departed. "One last thing," I ventured.

Hayes paused.

"If one of your patrols heads west toward my spread on the North Platte, could they let my wife know that I'm okay?"

"I'll see what I can do," were his parting words.

The surgeon shrugged, gave me a disdainful sort of look, and went about treating my wounds. "I'll say this, O'Toole. Whatever Injun cures you packed onto your wounds likely saved your life," he admitted grudgingly. I think he took pleasure in inflicting as much pain as possible, as he went on to cleaning my cuts. "No telling what sort of junk was on those bear claws," he said as he probed and scraped. "The bullet did you no favors either."

I forced a forgiving smile that likely looked more like a grimace.

The surgeon paused and stepped back. "I believe in our Maker, too, but you're going to need a lot of help from Him." He stitched the worst of my wounds as best he could, applied salves, and began to bandage my wounds. "If you get past the next couple of days with the infection subsiding, your arm will recover, son. You'll have some terrible scars but should have full use."

* * *

"Wake up," came a voice that seemed to come from far away.

I looked up into a broad smile framed in a Black face with lively eyes. "George?" I asked groggily.

"The surgeon says your arm is getting better. Awentia and the children know you're here," shared George Freeman in his deep baritone voice.

"Where are they?" I pressed.

"Waiting at home. We're wrangling you free of the sawbones today. We've got a nice, gentle wagon ready for you."

"I can come home already?"

"Shucks, Isa. You've been here four days."

I blinked. "That long?"

He nodded. "Captain Hayes sent a patrol out the day after you arrived here. We've been waiting for you to get strong enough to be carted home."

I raised my left arm and smiled. The color had returned to my hand, and the numbness was gone. "I'm ready," I said.

"Captain Hayes wants a few words with you before you leave," advised George. "He'll be along shortly."

As George spoke the words, Captain Hayes appeared in the doorway. "May I come in?"

He need not have asked. He was commandant of the fort, after all, but I appreciated his respect.

"I'm pleased to see that you're well enough to travel, Mr. O'Toole. We're all impressed that you survived those wounds. I understand those poultices were Comanche remedies. They surely saved you." He smiled with admiration. "I would like to know about those two horses you towed in with you."

I sighed. I knew that I'd eventually have to explain. "Two men tried to bushwhack me near the South Platte. One of them put a bullet through my shoulder before my wolf companion eliminated him. The second man charged at me with rifle blazing, but his horse tripped. He was thrown from his saddle and broke his neck. I buried the two and put their personal effects in the saddlebags."

"I took the liberty of looking in their saddlebags. Farley Degrange and Kyle Jones?" asked Hayes.

I nodded.

He gave me a penetrating look. "I feel as though there's more to this."

"True, Captain. I'd run into them in Palo Duro Canyon on my way south. They had been wranglers on the JA Ranch and been let go. They were up to no good." I paused to take a breath. My wounds still felt tight across my back. "The two coveted my horse and pack mule. I tried to convince them of the error of their ways and urged them to seek their fortunes legitimately in a place like Deadwood. I expect it was pure chance that they ran into me on the trail, as I was heading home. They reckoned to waylay me again."

"So, they sort of died from natural causes brought on by their own greedy intentions," observed George.

George was right. Taabe had killed one, and the second bushwhacker's horse had killed him. I had no hand in the death of either man. "I tried to set them on a straight path, but the way was too narrow for them with all their greed and bitterness. My pa told us that helping folks can be like tossing a stone into a pond, as you never know what obstacles the ripples might encounter."

Hayes scratched his head. "Guess it was God's will." He gave me an admiring look, glanced at George, and grew serious. "From examining that bearskin and the wounds on your back, you looked to have been right close and personal with that grizzly."

"Didn't have a choice, Captain." What else could I say? "That bear had sand." I smiled. I'd stated the obvious. But the difference was that the bear fought out of animal instinct, while my courage sprang from a rational decision to live.

Hayes laughed. "I doubt there's an ounce of fear in you, Mr. O'Toole."

"To the contrary, Captain. I'm much aware of fear, it can be a constant companion and rule us if we permit it. I try to learn, for my pa told me—and Mr. Freeman here is my witness—that knowledge triumphs over fear. We only fear what we fail to understand." I had no idea where my words came from. I suppose I sounded like quite a…a philosopher, I think they call it.

"As bad a shape as you were in, I'm impressed that you managed to skin that grizzly. You're going to be a legend here at Fort Laramie," Hayes said admiringly.

George just stood there smiling. Such outsized thoughts had arisen more than once, sitting at one of his after-dinner gatherings around the Freeman hearth. We'd discussed humbleness in the face of achievement.

The doc walked in. "Y'all going to stand around jawing or let this man go home?"

I suppose I should have felt that some progress had been made, as he described me as a man rather than a half-breed. I raised myself to a sitting position and swung my legs out from the bed. I pulled on my buck-skin pants and slipped into my moccasins. The doc draped a blanket over my naked shoulders. My wounds weren't quite ready to handle a shirt. My legs were in decent shape, so I managed to stand. "Well, what are we waiting for?" I turned to the surgeon. "Thanks, Major. I owe you a lot." The man had saved my arm. It was still stiff, but the color was back, and it would soon be good as new.

The doc simply nodded. "Don't overwork yourself for a couple of weeks," he advised and moved to leave the room.

I knew in my heart that he admired me; that he'd found space in his soul for me. "Thank you, Major." I shook his hand.

"You're all right, O'Toole," he finally said. "Pleased I could save that arm."

* * *

Outside the fort dispensary stood a wagon with Mukue and Bertrum tethered behind it. My saddle, saddlebags, guns, and the bearskin were piled in the wagon bed. Now, my thoughts began to focus more fully on Morning Star. I looked forward to her loving arms.

With my right arm draped over George's shoulder to steady my stride, we moved ever-so-gently to the wagon. I exchanged a knowing sort of look with Mukue as he and Bertrum stood tethered to the back of the wagon. Taabe was nowhere to be seen; not surprising given that most of the soldiers would be inclined toward killing wolves as predatory pests. George helped me into the wagon bed, and I found myself relieved to lie back comfortably on straw-filled bedding.

The soldiers at Fort Laramie, bless their souls, had taken it upon themselves to begin the bearskin tanning process by scraping the underside of any remnants of flesh and salting it. It would be a long process that I'd finish at home.

George climbed into the seat, gave a nicker to the horses, and off we went with a lurch that I felt to my bones. I said nothing.

As we departed the fort, I peeked over the sides of the wagon. Three gate guards saluted as we went by. I wasn't sure it was deserved, but I appreciated the respect.

CHAPTER 3

RECOVERY

Home! George pulled the rig up to the front door. Morning Star had heard the jingling of the harnesses, so stood waiting at our door with Moses at her feet and Michael in her arms. Chester Donovan and our ranch hands, Will Cutter and Joe Moon, stood at the corral.

I managed to sit up and throw the boys a smile, at which Moses began to cry. I suppose my appearance was a tad scary. My hair was disheveled, one eye still bore discoloration from a bruise, and the blanket draped over my shoulder wasn't up to covering all of my ugly, still-healing wounds.

Morning Star soothed Moses as best she could and glided over to the wagon.

George climbed down, and he and Chester gently eased me to the ground.

Morning Star's and my eyes locked.

"I'm home," I said.

Tears began to stream down my warrior wife's cheeks as she let Moses to the ground and moved to me.

My arms encircled her. My tender wounds ignored

the hurt from her hand wrapped around my back. There were no words. I was home. Morning Star was in my arms. Gazing into her eyes, I saw the truth in there being people you can live with, but only one whom you can't live without.

We began to walk toward the house, when I had to stop. I turned to Donovan. "Chester, just let Mukue run free. You'll never get him in a stall. He'll be back when I'm ready for him." With that, Morning Star and I walked hand in hand into our home. George followed with my saddle bags, my guns, and the huge bearskin.

Morning Star helped ease me onto the bench at our kitchen table. "Awentia happy her man is home," she said. She released my hand and fetched the coffee pot. "Come, George. Sit," she invited. "Thank you for bringing Isa home."

George smiled and took a sip of coffee. "Your pa would be proud, Isa." It was about the twentieth time he'd said that since picking me up at Fort Laramie. Maybe not twenty, but he couldn't get it out of his head that I'd survived a bushwhacking and a bear attack.

"I'll tell everyone about it after dinner," I responded. I turned tenderly to Morning Star, "What of Spotted Elk?" I asked.

"My father is with God," she replied reverently.

I hadn't meant to throw cold water on the celebration of my homecoming, but I had to know. He had seemed pretty weak when I departed for Texas. After all, the condition of her father had been the reason Morning Star didn't accompany me to Texas. "With God?" I asked.

"He see happiness you bring here and decide he like God."

George and I exchanged glances. I felt an inner peace that Spotted Elk would await us in heaven. "And the *numunuu?*" I asked, wondering what became of the Lakota accompanying Spotted Elk.

"Go Standing Rock," she replied.

I knew that the Standing Rock Agency was one of five agencies that comprised the Great Sioux Reservation established by the Fort Laramie Treaty of 1868. The treaty was now hardly worth the paper it had been printed on, as it had been broken by both sides many times in the ensuing years. They at least had a place to go.

Moses had by now accommodated my scary-looking appearance and yielded to his inbred attraction for me. He leaned against my leg and simply stared up into my face. I smiled and tousled his hair. "Your pa is home, son," I said.

"How wounds?" asked Morning Star.

"They hurt some. The Army surgeon saved my arm. Said the poultices you packed in my saddlebags helped."

She stood, gently raised the blanket from my shoulders, and looked at my wounds. "Bullet, too?" She hadn't been told about the bushwhacking.

I nodded. "Happened about five days south of Fort Laramie. All on the same day."

She went to the cupboard and found a loose-fitting tunic. With her help, I managed to slip into it.

"That's better," I said gratefully. The weight of the blanket had been uncomfortable, so the tunic was a relief. It also afforded me greater freedom of motion.

She ran her fingers through my shaggy hair, gave me a light kiss, and blushed as she caught George watching with his trademark smile.

"Maybe, I ought to be moseying, folks," offered George. "Let y'all catch up private like."

I caught Morning Star's eyes. She nodded for George to stay.

"Thanks for your help, my friend," I said. "We would like you to join us for dinner. *Ana o'a hi'it.*" I threw in the Comanche invitation to lighten the conversation.

George laughed. "I would like to hear the story of the bear from your lips, Isa."

"We'll invite the ranch hands in after dinner. Might as well get through it once." I lifted Moses onto my lap.

He curiously touched the wounds on my arm.

"Careful. They hurt," I said affectionately.

Moses pulled his little paw back and looked up at me with a smile. "Pa," he said.

The thought that bushwhackers and a grizzly nearly took me away from this brought tears to the corners of my eyes.

"Pa," he repeated.

"Awentia get dinner," said Morning Star with a soft smile.

Given all the adventures she and I experienced, I don't recall ever appreciating her so much as in this very moment. I looked forward to a vast improvement in my condition after weeks on the trail, and especially the chow during my stay at Fort Laramie. Army food was simply lacking.

"Isa?" George cut into my daydreaming. "Have you heard about Sitting Bull?"

I shook my head. I'd heard rumors through my groggy recovery at Fort Laramie, but no solid information. It had been years since I'd met the Hunkpapa Lakota chief.

George took a sip of coffee. "Canada became uncomfortable for him and his people. They were hungry and beginning to get desperate over their survival. Sitting

Bull led his family and followers back to the United States and surrendered at Fort Buford. I understand that he had his son Crow Foot surrender the great chief's rifle to the fort's commanding officer. It was reported that the chief defiantly told the major in command something like, '*I wish it to be remembered that I was the last man of my tribe to surrender my rifle.*' The Army celebrated the surrender, but I don't think it will be the last we hear of Sitting Bull." George took another sip of coffee and put his cup down with a sort of finality.

"Tatanka Iyotake brave chief. Great leader," said Morning Star, looking over her shoulder from her cooking.

"Spotted Elk's family joined Sitting Bull," I observed, as that's where his people headed after leaving Laramie Cross Breed Ranch.

"In Texas, the Comanche have gone to reservations in Oklahoma Territory. The Apache make trouble at the border with Mexico." I took a deep breath and fondled my coffee cup thoughtfully. "Would that all *numunuu* could live in peace. It is what God would have us do."

"Folks need the truth," rejoined George.

Morning Star turned from her cooking. "I believe truth. Some think there are other truths."

My warrior wife had become a philosopher. "Many truths are illusions…slippery, subtle, deceitful. It is good to suspect those who claim to know the truth until we know the truth they declare." I could wax philosophically, as well.

George sat back and laughed. "I am in the company of deep thinkers, sages. Yet, you've both found *the truth*."

Soon, we found ourselves enjoying a satisfying meal of elk and all manner of side dishes cooked at Morning Star's whim. We avoided conversation about my return journey from Texas, though I was pleased to share how the beginnings of our cattle enterprise were in place, thanks to August Klappenbach and my pa.

With dinner finished, we invited Donovan, Cutter, and Moon to join us around the hearth to hear of the part of my adventure that left me on the precipice of death. I was never one for long stories about myself. In the telling of the bushwhacking and the bear attack, I gave credit to God for His protection. By this time, Taabe had found his way home. He joined the hearth circle and raised his head and gave a soft yip upon mention of his helping battle the grizzly. How did he know that I'd mentioned him? Like my pa with his wolf companion, Zeb, I had learned not to question God's divine purpose in bringing Taabe to me.

Once I had finished telling my tale, it seemed that everyone figured that I deserved private time with my family, especially Morning Star. As bad a shape as I was still in, I wasn't sure what they expected.

* * *

We did find ourselves alone at last. The children were sleeping, George had headed home under a starlit sky, and our ranch hands were enjoying the creature comforts of the bunkhouse. Morning Star and I found ourselves standing face-to-face at the hearth.

I took her hands in mine and gazed deeply into her eyes. Ah, those beautiful eyes set above those golden-bronzed cheeks, her delicate aquiline nose. Love poured through my being. "You saved my life."

She gave me a questioning look as if to say how, as she had been nowhere near me during the attacks.

"I mean, you kept me alive after the battles." My

words flowed lovingly. "You were ever in my thoughts as I fought to reach the fort."

Still, her eyes spoke questioningly.

"I lived for you, Awentia. You kept me alive."

She stood on tiptoe and kissed me softly. "God keep Isa alive for Awentia," she murmured.

My wounds mattered not as I drew her tightly to me. Her lips beckoned. Our passion flowed through to the very cores of our beings. "You are the one I cannot live without," I assured her.

Morning Star's kiss was akin to heaven.

* * *

I was left mostly to my personal musings as I recuperated. I wasn't up to ranch chores. Donovan retrieved the much-dog-eared copy of *The Deerslayer* from my saddlebags, and I told him I'd read it on my journey. I promised myself to return the book to Guernsey as soon as I was able. I found myself beginning to yearn for book knowledge, and I reckoned to borrow more books from Guernsey's library.

It had occurred to me that in knowledge, there was power that no physical weapon could replicate. My knowledge of the frontier had enabled Morning Star and me to meet the challenges of our escape from Bull Elk and was enabling us to raise the finest Quarter Horses. Unlike rifles and bows and arrows, knowledge could never be lost. Fires, floods, storms, and battles happened, but the content of our minds was forever ours. I had come to realize that civilization was advanced through curiosity. Ignorance was not bliss. It further occurred to me that so many in our midst feared free speech, flagellating themselves in a paradox of shame. Many dropped

God by the wayside, unaware that lack of moral grounding is a fool's game.

The long, lonely ride from Texas had given me plenty of time to ponder life. I'd read *The Deerslayer* four times on the trip south and felt as though I knew it from memory. Young Bumppo, known as *Deerslayer* among the Delaware tribe with whom he lived, helped the trapper Thomas Hutter to resist an attack by the Iroquois hostiles who were allied with the French. It was a tale often repeated by other cultures across the centuries.

Resting gave my mind the opportunity to wander. I wasn't on some unfamiliar trail demanding that I be alert for lurking threats. I read our Bible, but found myself striving to probe its depths. My ma and pa had taught us from its pages, and our friend George reinforced the Word here in Wyoming, but I feared being held captive to the dogma of any particular version of Christianity or any faith for that matter. I yearned to learn more of dogma, as it often seemed wrong even among those of no religious faith.

I rejected the idea of being spoon-fed knowledge from those who sought to control me through its application. Just as we'd seen in the War Between the States, the Comanche wars, and the Plains Indians Wars, generations of those in power seek to impose their will on people's lives. In my observation, dogma creates an inert, stagnant pattern in its followers that stifles imagination, rejects questioning of authority, and becomes an intensely powerful excuse for violence against challengers.

My thoughts were running heavy. I hoped Guernsey might have some books on what was called philosophy. I ached to open my mind. To hone my mind's edge would take absorbing knowledge from the teachings of others. It occurred to me that while a stone sharpened a knife and fire tempered steel, it took men to sharpen men.

As I sat at our kitchen table, I turned to Morning Star. "I aim to visit Mr. Guernsey soon. I must return his book." There was a tone of implication in my voice. "Perhaps, you could join me."

"And?" asked Morning Star.

"I wish to learn more," I replied. "He has books I yearn to read, to learn from."

"Are not the valleys and mountains and waters enough? Have you not learned all there is from the mountain lion and the bear? Have you not gained knowledge of the people?" As her questions spewed forth, I sensed her beginning to answer them with my ultimate question. Could we ever learn enough? Finally, she sat back and gazed inquiringly into my eyes as though probing deep within my mind. "What of the Holy Book?"

"I think God gave us the ability to journey beyond His Bible. I wish to pursue that journey."

"Awentia go with Isa," she said firmly. She'd decided that it wouldn't do to have her husband go on this journey alone.

CHAPTER 4

SPIRIT HORSE

I had lazed around the house for a total of four days. Morning Star treated my still-healing wounds with medicines from Fort Laramie as well as her very own Lakota medicinal poultices. I began to take walks, venturing a bit further each day.

On the fifth day home, I found Mukue awaiting me at the corral gate. I gave him a sugar treat and plenty of the sort of affection only found between a man and his cayuse. I reckoned to ride him in another day or so.

Morning Star and I had begun making plans for our journey to The Emigrant's Washtub and Charles Guernsey's house. We even decided to bring a Quarter Horse to gift him as a sign of our commitment to future trade and neighborliness. Now, it was a matter of my wounds having healed sufficiently for travel.

On the morning of the seventh day of my wound-imposed captivity, I stepped from our front door to behold a warrior's pony standing not ten yards from me. For a moment, I thought it was an apparition, a specter. Then, he whinnied, snorted, and nodded his head. I didn't reckon a spirit to be making such sounds. The war pony was a dusty white, his hide emblazoned with faded symbols traced in yellow and red. Time-worn black paint encircled its eyes like spectacles designed to sharpen its vision. Three rain-streaked yellow lines were stacked across his nose. A red handprint on his shoulder told that his rider had been out for blood. A saddle was strapped to his back.

For all I knew, the pony might well have been ridden into a battle. Where was its rider? We stared at each other for a few moments, then he ambled a bit hesitantly toward me. An eerie feeling swept over me as though some spirit of the past had been set before me. "What are you telling me, God?" I asked in a whisper.

He finally stopped within arm's length. I reached out to stroke his nose, but he shied away. We stood eye to eye for what seemed an interminable time. I slowly reached out my hand. Ever-so-slowly, he extended his snout and nuzzled my hand. I examined the saddle and judged it to be of Lakota making.

Morning Star appeared in the doorway with Michael in her arms.

What I now thought of as a spirit horse perked up, backed away from me, and pranced a bit before walking over to Morning Star. He didn't hesitate, even bumping her gently with his nose. Baby Michael squealed with delight and patted the pony's nose.

"I think Awentia has a friend," I observed.

About this time, Mukue trotted from around the corner of the house. He stopped to survey the scene. I looked from him to the spirit horse. Would the two stallions accept each other?

The answer came swiftly, as Mukue walked over to me and rested his nose on my shoulder as if to claim me as his. This was a relief, though not so much a surprise. After all, we had several Quarter Horse stallions that Mukue was used to. That thought of the Quarter Horses reminded me that our ranch continued to grow. We had several two-year-olds that would be ready for sale come spring. We would prepare for that over the winter. This spirit pony would likely not be bred but serve as personal transportation.

"We keep pony?" Morning Star's question brought me back to the here and now.

"Awentia ride instead of the mare?" The spirit horse was bigger and looked to be younger than the mare she'd been riding. Both were battle-tested, so either would be more than adequate for riding the frontier. It still puzzled me as to what might have become of the pony's rider.

Morning Star nodded. "*Akicita sukawaka,*" she said in the Lakota tongue. This was a warrior horse.

I nodded. "Where *akicita*?" I asked with a shrug.

Morning Star saw dried blood on the saddle. "*Akicita kte,*" she replied, pointing to the blood stain.

The rider had apparently been killed or wounded, and his pony escaped in the midst of the chaos of battle. "I wonder whether he'll take one of our saddles?"

"We try. Ride him to visit Mr. Guernsey."

I reckoned that was doable. The Emigrant's Washtub wasn't that far, and it would be a good test. The spirit horse was certainly strong enough to handle Morning Star, along with Moses and Michael mounted in cradle-boards draped behind the saddle. As I considered this, Morning Star handed Michael to me and began leading the stallion to the stable.

"Awentia wash away war paint," she advised as I watched her lead him away. Tender loving care was surely in his future. As to the war paint, I suppose it could be said that there was a certain symbolism in the pony having found his way out of battle and coming upon a place with people he could trust.

* * *

It was a great feeling to be making the short journey to The Emigrant's Washtub with my family. We were confident that Donovan and our two new hands had ranch operations under control. I was now nearly fully healed from my encounters with the bushwhackers and the bear. Life seemed good, God was good.

I'd washed the paint from the spirit horse. In fact, we wound up naming him Wamaka Nagi Sukawaka, or Spirit Horse. He was a beautiful stallion, even at a little better than a hand smaller than Mukue. Once we'd evaluated his temperament, we'd decide whether he was suitable for breeding with the Quarter Horses.

I cut out a two-year-old Quarter Horse as a gift for Guernsey. My plan was to use the gift to cement our business relationship. Last but hardly least, we packed our trusty mule Bertrum with camping necessities and a few trade goods in case we had an opportunity to do a bit of bartering.

Our little caravan headed out early. I reckoned to make Guernsey's before midday. Our plan was to enjoy the afternoon, spend the night, and head home the next morning.

CHAPTER 5

GUERNSEY'S LIBRARY

Blessedly, our travel to The Emigrant's Washtub was uneventful. We sighted a distant grizzly, a small herd of elk, several deer, and a couple of eagles. We were ever appreciative of our natural surroundings. Notably, the handful of rattlesnakes that we spotted managed to stay clear of our trail.

When the grizzly had come into view, Morning Star looked curiously at me, "Isa no fear?"

I smiled. Bear encounters were a given here on the Wyoming frontier. While I'd defeated one grizzly, I had no desire to take on another. Nevertheless, I felt no fear. "No fear," I said and patted my new bear claw necklace. I knew that so long as humans left the big bears alone, they'd pretty much ignore us. Trouble only came when the bears felt threatened.

Following the North Platte River was a convenient route, as it led us directly to The Emigrant's Washtub and Guernsey's ranch.

"River beautiful," observed Morning Star.

That was a hint. We stopped to take a break and

stood arm in arm, admiring God's handiwork. Little Moses ran about, though he was wary of the river. Michael remained in his cradleboard but soon drew our attention with a hunger cry.

As we turned to meet his needs, I caught sight of a bobcat stalking Moses. The cat was on a rock near the riverbank about thirty feet from him. Focused yellow eyes and twitching tail hinted at his plan despite our presence. Was he so hungry that he figured to make off with a small child before we could react? I pulled my Spencer carbine, levered a round into the chamber, and squeezed off a shot that hit a rock mere inches from the bobcat's nose. He sprinted off as fast as his paws could carry him.

Moses was momentarily stunned at the sound of my rifle, but quickly recovered and calmly walked over to us. He was on a path to grow up as fearless.

The bobcat threat served as a reminder to be ever on guard. It did serve to break our quiet moment of appreciating God's creation. We mounted up and continued our journey to The Emigrant's Washtub.

The incident with the bobcat got me back to thinking on the killing of game. I resented the needless slaughter of buffalo, such as was undertaken during the visit of a Russian royal back in 1872, and subsequent wiping out of herds by buffalo hunters. Yet a reasonable amount of hunting made sense toward conserving certain wild game populations. There was also a long-standing connection between hunting and manhood. My White ancestors and Comanche ancestors considered a boy's first hunt as part of the introduction into manhood. So far as I was concerned, we men were hunter-gatherers. Then again, there seemed a driving need to control the frontier environment to attract the ranches, farms, and towns that marked civilization.

* * *

Guernsey's modest house soon came into view. Our journey had been without incident save for scaring off the bobcat. It had been great to travel as a family, and there was something about riding horses and just enjoying the crisp mountain air that offered a sense of freedom.

Guernsey's house wasn't far from Register Cliff, a travel landmark at which pioneers heading west often stopped to carve their names, initials, and dates in the limestone rock. Guernsey even blasted a hole at the cliff base for a cool, dry chamber to store potatoes. As with many places along the Oregon Trail, there were a few unmarked graves that Guernsey respectfully left undisturbed. I suppose that served as a measure of the man.

We figured to stop at Guernsey's place upon arrival. I saw it as a matter of courtesy before finding a place for us to set up our camp for the night.

We reined in in front of his house. I'd just dismounted and was helping Morning Star from her saddle when Guernsey opened his front door and peered out at us. "That you, O'Toole?" he said by way of greeting. "Where you been, my friend, and who's that with you?"

"Good to see you, Mr. Guernsey." By now, he'd found his way to us and was vigorously shaking my hand. "This is my wife Awentia, and our sons Moses and Michael."

"Well, pleased to meet y'all. Come on in, and I'll brew up some coffee." His eyes went to the Quarter Horse we'd brought. He cocked his head at me in a questioning manner.

"Just a gift for you. Hope you don't think it too bold of me."

Guernsey walked over and affectionately patted the stallion's nose and stroked his neck. "What a fine bit of horseflesh, Isa. Thank you kindly. I haven't begun ranching operations yet, but we can talk of that later." He paused. "I'm sorry, Mrs. O'Toole. I didn't mean to ignore you or the little ones. Welcome to my abode. Why don't you go straight inside and make yourselves comfortable while Isa and I stable these horses and the mule." He took a step, then paused again. "You will be staying in my home?" he suggested invitingly.

Morning Star smiled affectionately. "Thank you," she responded. With that, she lifted the boys from Spirit Horse and headed inside.

I accompanied Guernsey and our mounts to his stable.

"It's been a challenge to get ranching operations underway. It seems big investment money has settled on Cheyenne. With its railroads and stockyards, it's become a hub. I've sent a couple of folks out to buy some cattle, though I think I found the beginnings of a herd with a herd from a Black fellow down the river a piece."

"You've met my friend George Freeman?" I asked with a smile. "He's a dear friend of ours."

"He's a talker, too. Told quite a story about escaping slavery and making a life for himself up here as a rancher. Guess he ranched the North Platte country before it was discovered." Guernsey unsaddled Spirit Horse and began currying him while I took care of Mukue. "I've already learned a thing or two from

Freeman about ranching up here where the winters can be brutal."

"George is pretty savvy," I observed.

"Where have you been?" asked Guernsey.

"Went to my pa's ranch down in Texas to look into the cattle business. It sure seems to be booming everywhere. I hear tell that there's plenty of money to be made." I responded.

"You after the big money, Isa?" pressed Guernsey.

"Only hope to earn enough for a comfortable life for my family. I love the horses and cattle and the ruggedness of the frontier and reckon to make a life from it. I think that as you get a lot of money, you tend to be owned by it. I don't need or want a big fancy house or stylish clothes. I expect that, if I went to see the President of these United States, I'd wear my buckskins and moccasins." I hoisted the pack from Bertrum over my shoulder, and we headed back to the house.

Morning Star had gotten settled in by the time we returned from the stable. Typical of the hospitality of the frontier west, she'd started the coffee brewing and joined us at the kitchen table. "You have fine home, Mr. Guernsey," she offered.

"Thank you kindly. Since we're all friends, feel free to call me Charles," responded Guernsey.

Morning Star smiled. "I am Awentia. Is Lakota for Morning Star." She arose and fetched the coffee pot.

Guernsey watched Morning Star fill our cups, nodded his thanks, and then turned to me. "Has George Freeman mentioned the Wyoming Stock Growers Association to you, Isa?" he asked.

"I've heard of it, but George has never mentioned it. It's based in Cheyenne, isn't it?" I replied.

"Some big cattlemen founded it a few years back. I've

heard rumors that they were resenting what they call the intrusion of small ranches and farms. The association sees them as restricting the range and limiting access to water and the best grasses," observed Guernsey.

I looked thoughtfully into my coffee cup. "Resentment can get out of hand," I observed. "Did George say whether he was joining up? He's got a good-sized spread and likes to keep his ear to the ground."

"Some big-money Harvard investors control the association. They're cattlemen only by way of putting money in big spreads here in Wyoming."

I laughed. "So, they don't get their boots muddy?"

Guernsey chuckled and sipped his coffee.

"Talking with George recently, he observed that there are makers and takers in this world," I postulated.

"You mean folks that work hard to build things versus those that reap the bounty of the builders' efforts." Guernsey savored a sip of his coffee and turned to Morning Star. "Awentia, you brewed this coffee better than I ever did. You'll have to show me how you did it."

"Maybe Laramie Cross Breed Ranch join Wyoming Stock Growers Association," she contributed.

"Might not be a bad idea, Isa. Awentia makes good sense," suggested Guernsey.

I nodded. We were already considering buying out our neighbor Connor Culthwaite, as he was struggling to support his family. Culthwaite spoke of heading to Buffalo, up in Johnson County, to set up a blacksmith business. The lush valleys east of the Bighorn Mountains were attracting cattlemen and the cowboys whose horses needed to be shod. Acquiring his land would give us better than two thousand acres. Joining the association would tie us in to the goings on of the cattle industry and connect us with Quarter Horse buyers. I had a feeling that the bigger cattle operations might become concerned enough about the incursion of smaller ranches and farms to take the law into their own hands.

Then, I had to question the existence of the law in Wyoming. If the cattlemen got too big for their britches, they could become enemies. "We will join this Wyoming Stock Growers Association, Charles." That was decided. It did feel a little strange to have begun calling Guernsey by his first name. I suppose I'd get used to it. I felt as though his commitment to Wyoming would lead him into politics.

"Joining would be smart. I reckon to do so myself. I don't trust big-money college men. The association founders belong to the exclusive Cheyenne Club, and I think they pretty much own the editorial thinking of the Cheyenne newspapers. I'm not so sure I'd trust everything I read in the *Cheyenne Daily Sun*." Guernsey paused thoughtfully for a moment.

"Speaking of reading, I brought *The Deerslayer* back to return to your library. I read it a few times on my ride to Texas."

"Pleased that you enjoyed it, Isa. Maybe you and Awentia both would like to borrow from my library." He suggested.

Morning Star perked up at the implied recognition of her intellectual capacity. Sad to say, women had yet to achieve equality across America, not to mention the frontier. If not married, women on the frontier tended to hold menial jobs, and many were sucked into the web of prostitution, usually to their eventual ruin. Here in Wyoming, Morning Star held respect as my wife among open-minded folk, yet there were those who discounted her as a Lakota squaw. Those same people held my being a half-breed as something lower than the snakes. So it was that I valued Guernsey's hospitality and appreciated his respect despite our heritage. "Have you added new books?" I asked.

He nodded. "Borrow as many as you like. You might especially appreciate *Two Treatises of Government* by a fellow named John Locke. I hear tell his writings influenced our Declaration of Independence."

Guernsey's suggestion intrigued me. My pa had introduced us to a couple of Greek philosophers, but I sought to expand my knowledge. Learning beyond Aristotle and Plato held some appeal.

"Why don't y'all settle in and enjoy the library while my cook wrestles us up some dinner?" suggested Guernsey.

Morning Star and I wasted no time finding our way to our host's collection of books.

"This looks good," said Morning Star, as she gently leafed through the pages of a book by a man named George Belden called *Twelve Years Among the Wild Indians of the Plains*.

I thought it was an ambitious read for her to undertake. "Are you sure?"

"I read *The Deerslayer* while you sleep," she chided. "I wish to read what White man say about our people."

I couldn't disagree and had to admire her curiosity. I found the John Locke book Guernsey had mentioned, then found myself turning the pages of a book by an Army general named Lew Wallace. It was a heavy volume and titled *Ben Hur*. It having been set in the time of early Christianity caught my attention. Apparently, this Ben Hur fellow had to endure much pain and suffering in his pursuit of truth. Given my own vision quest in search of life purpose, I reckoned I might learn something from Wallace's writings.

"Y'all hungry?" Guernsey poked his head in.

* * *

We followed him to a room off the kitchen for dining. Guernsey wasn't much of a decorator, but he'd spared no expense in furnishing the room with mahogany paneling and beautiful oak furniture of French design but American-built. Our place settings were of fine China set off with silver flatware, crystal goblets, and lace napkins. The bowls of vegetables and a platter of sliced beef and another of warm buttery biscuits had me salivating before I'd even put a morsel to my mouth. We took our seats, then paused to look expectantly at our host.

Guernsey already had a juicy piece of beef ready to pop into his mouth when he realized that we hadn't lifted a fork or knife. An *ah-ha* expression swept across his face. He placed his fork back onto his plate. "Let's bless our meal," he said.

The blessing was brief and further cemented the respect I held for Guernsey. He was a gracious host and was obviously sensitive to our beliefs, assuming he fully understood them.

* * *

Morning Star and I settled Moses before taking an after-dinner walk. Little Michael fussed enough that she put him in the cradleboard and took him with us. I did carry my Colt revolver in a holster on my hip. Out here, a person quickly learns that not everyone is a friend, plus there is no telling what sort of varmint might be encountered.

The Emigrant's Washtub, with its gathering of

settlers headed westward on the Oregon Trail, was close enough to visit, so that's where we headed. The place served as a resting spot before they tackled the mountains. They repaired anything that needed fixing, bathed in the North Platte River, and enjoyed time off the trail that already had been their home for weeks. They'd come from all sorts of places, including Europe, and tended to bring with them whatever culture they'd lived with. I didn't envy wagon masters the task of keeping order among often very diverse groups of travelers.

As we drew near, a grizzled old-timer raised himself up from repairing a wagon axle. "Dang, but now we got us Injuns!" he groused.

We didn't pay him any attention, but it did remind us that we probably appeared as people that many of these folks feared. They'd undoubtedly heard tales of attacks, and some might have even experienced a run-in with rogue Indians that had spurned the reservations.

"You Redskins payin' me no never mind?" challenged the old man.

We might have simply walked on, but now the man lifted his rifle and began to brandish it a bit threateningly.

"We're peaceful, mister. Just out for a walk." I kept my hands away from my gun to show that we weren't aiming to cause any trouble.

"Dang, if it ain't Injuns what speak English," he observed sarcastically.

A couple of nearby folks heard the old man and stepped forward from their work. "You havin' a problem with these here Injuns, Willie?" asked a younger man. He was shorter than me, but well-muscled. He was unarmed save for an axe he'd been using to chop firewood.

I hoped these folks realized that we were no threat.

Other than my gun and knife, we carried nothing threatening. Plus, Michael was innocently sleeping in the cradleboard strapped to Morning Star's back. "We mean you no harm. We are guests of Mr. Guernsey back at yonder house." I motioned toward Guernsey's place.

"Only good Injun is a dead one!" threatened the old man with a toothless smile.

It was then that I noticed the yellow stripe running down his pant leg. The man had been a soldier. I thought that he might have had a bad experience fighting Indians. "I scouted for Colonel Stanley on the Yellowstone," I ventured in an attempt to establish some sort of connection.

"Yuh likely helped kill Custer," he responded.

The man with the axe moved a few steps away from the woman beside him and glared at us.

By now, the confrontation was beginning to grab some attention from other settlers. I overheard two fearful-looking men conversing in what I believed was German.

"Any more of yuh Redskins out thar?" asked the man we now figured was Willie. He slipped his finger over the rifle trigger. Willie hadn't aimed it at us just yet, but I was wary.

"Yuh say somethin' 'bout dead Injuns, Willie?" queried the axe man with a sinister grin.

The situation was heating up, and I desperately sought an escape. I surely didn't want to hurt anybody, not to mention the escalated risk to Morning Star, Michael, and myself. I signaled subtly to Morning Star to begin backing away toward Guernsey's house. We had managed a couple of steps when Willie fired his rifle into the air. Morning Star and I recoiled with surprise.

"Whar yuh goin'?" he challenged us.

I was seriously thinking about drawing my gun before Willie could lever another round into his rifle. Again, I held back. I simply didn't want these settlers' blood on my hands. "Don't fire that rifle again," I stated firmly.

"Yuh don't give me no orders, Injun," responded Willie. He began to aim the rifle toward me. He'd not yet chambered a round.

Just then, a bullet hit the wagon tongue, sending splinters flying. The report of the rifle was heard a split second later. From the sound and the damage it did to the wood, I was sure it was a Sharps buffalo gun.

"Leave those two alone!" hollered Guernsey from a hundred or so yards away.

By now, at least a dozen settlers had gathered. A couple of the men held rifles at the ready.

"Injun lover!" hollered Willie. He levered a round and pointed the muzzle toward me. "Git yur squaw outta here!" he said with an angry grimace that said he hated Indians but wasn't up to losing his life over it.

I kept my hand away from the Colt in my holster so as not to appear threatening to anyone.

"Put up your guns!" hollered Guernsey from afar.

Call it an accident if you will, but Willie squeezed off another round. The bullet ricocheted from the wooden top of the cradleboard that held Michael and plowed through my hat, grazing my skull as it passed by. That was far too close to my wife and son.

A split second later, two shots rang out. The first was from my Colt revolver that fired a bullet through Willie's shoulder, while the second came from Guernsey's Sharps and blew a chunk of Willie's posterior away. Willie was lucky that my aim was off, because I was of a mind to kill him in defense of my family.

The settlers were horrified. Mouths gaped, while Willie groveled with pain in the Wyoming dust.

I didn't even realize that I'd been hit. I wrapped my arm protectively around Morning Star and Michael while making a sweeping gesture with my gun as a warning to anyone looking to copy Willie's poor judgment. "We came in peace, and y'all made trouble. Put up your guns." I locked onto the eyes of the man with the axe. "The axe, too. Drop it," I added.

Everyone complied. So much for our peaceful walk to The Emigrant's Washtub.

"You," I said, pointing to one of the men. "See to Willie here before he bleeds out."

The man raised his hands and ran over to Willie.

Upon realizing the severity of Willie's wounds, Morning Star stepped free of my arm. "Man need medicine. I get." With that, she dropped Michael and the cradleboard beside me and headed at a run back to Guernsey's house to fetch poultices and bandages. She gave nary a glance as she passed Guernsey, who was walking toward us with his rifle ready to shoot again.

I stood in amazement for a moment, then realized her response was best. Perhaps, saving Willie would heal old resentments.

Guernsey arrived with an eye to fending off trouble. "Sorry about this, Isa. There's no accounting for the sort of trash those wagons bring along," apologized Guernsey.

"It's okay, Charles. Yonder shooter is carrying some sort of hurt deep inside...and now outside." I doffed my hat and ran my fingers through my hair. Glancing at my hand, I, for the first time, realized that I was bleeding just a bit. "Guess he nearly got me," I said with a calmness that had a chilling effect on the settlers.

Willie was moaning with pain as the settler carried out my direction to comfort him.

"Get some pressure on those wounds," I ordered. "He'll bleed out if you don't."

Morning Star returned from fetching materials with which to doctor Willie. She kneeled beside the wounded man.

The expression on Willie's face as he looked up at a Lakota woman tending to him was a conflicted mix of pleading for relief and his old prejudice.

"Pull down pants," she directed the settler whom I'd sent to comfort Willie.

The man hesitated at taking orders from an Indian, much less a woman.

"Are you deaf, man? You heard her," I upbraided.

He looked around disconcertedly before reluctantly pulling Willie's pants from his backside to reveal a bleeding mass of flesh. Guernsey's shot had indeed excised a fair-sized piece of the man's butt. A couple of inches over, and Willie never would have walked again... if he survived.

Morning Star went to work cleansing the wound before applying a poultice. She soon pretty much stopped the bleeding from Willie's backside and bandaged it. Now, she went to work on the wound I'd put in his shoulder. Fortunately for Willie, my bullet had passed clean through the fleshy part of his shoulder and missed bone. She applied more poultice and bandaged him up.

Willie wouldn't be especially useful over the next couple of weeks, but it appeared that he would recover. He'd surely begin to have second thoughts on how he felt about Indians, given that his life had likely just been saved by one. The wounded man lay on his side, as he wouldn't be doing any sitting for a while. He looked over at me. He tried to find words, but wasn't quite able to bring himself to thank Morning Star. However, he looked as though he might be done with his Indian-hating days.

Morning Star shared some poultice and bandages with one of the settler women in a gesture of kindness.

By now, there were better than two dozen settlers who'd heard the gunfire and gathered around. Those who'd actually witnessed Willie's aggression and the outcome whispered their accounts to newcomers. Guernsey still had his Sharps rifle at the ready, though I'd holstered my Colt. I scanned the crowd, making eye contact with as many as possible. "You folks take good care of Willie here. Have safe travels to Oregon."

As if on cue, Taabe appeared. He walked over and nuzzled my hand, much to the amazement of onlookers.

Willie struggled to rise on an elbow. "You ain't no ordinary Injun. Who you be?" he asked, fighting through his pain.

"Isa O'Toole," I said it firmly enough that he'd never forget.

He looked at me through red-rimmed, pain-laden eyes. "Sorry I made yuh trouble." With that, he passed out. It appeared that Willie had overcome some of his prejudice.

I'd nearly forgotten my own minor wound until Morning Star came over and dabbed at it with a little of her poultice concoction. "Looks as though everything has worked out," I observed.

She nodded. "God good."

"You lead a charmed life, Isa O'Toole," said Guernsey, as he finally put up his rifle and gazed at the splintered top of the cradleboard and the hole in my hat.

I could have shared the many times in my short life that I'd been in dire straits and somehow managed to survive. "The Lord watches over me," I said simply.

We headed back to Guernsey's house. I looked back at the scene of our encounter and noted that the setting sun was causing the first shadows to move away from the forest walls. Register Cliff was already engulfed in shade. It was all right beautiful to behold.

* * *

Next morning, it was a welcome relief to sit in Guernsey's study and sip coffee. Morning Star was off caring for Moses and Michael, so he and I had some time for just the two of us. I worked on finishing repairs to the cradleboard as we conversed.

"I'm worried about what the future holds, Isa," shared Guernsey. "Those cattle ranch investors from Europe worry me. They're gentlemen of breeding and don't know an honest day's labor."

"Seems they've mostly stayed away from Texas. My pa mentioned no concern. I do worry for smaller ranches like George's here in Wyoming, though he's surely up to defending himself should anyone try to chase him out. I expect they'll not bother me, since my Quarter Horses don't compete with their cattle other than my access to the North Platte and Laramie Rivers."

"You'd do well to join the association, Isa." He paused and looked at me. "If they'll have you," he added ruefully.

That comment was telling. He knew that prejudice ran deep among the monied cattlemen of Wyoming. I was determined to ask George whether he'd tried to join the association. If they'd accepted a Black man, might I have a chance?

"Oh, and I'd like to buy a couple of those fine Quarter Horses you're breeding. I want my cowboys to ride only the best horses. How does five hundred dollars a head sound?"

I tried not to show surprise. Guernsey's offer was generous. I knew that I could get more in Cheyenne, but his ranch being close by saved me the cost and time for transporting the horses to market. "You've got a deal, Charles. When would you like us to deliver them?"

His barn wasn't quite ready, so we decided to hold the horses over the winter at Laramie Cross Breed Ranch.

* * *

Long about mid-morning, Morning Star and I were packed and ready to head home. It had been a worthwhile trip both in terms of cementing a friendship with Guernsey and agreeing upon our first Quarter Horse transaction. He had only just begun his Guernsey Cattle Company ranch there near Register Cliff, but it would surely be taking full advantage of the growing demand for beef.

The dust-up with the folks at The Emigrant's Washtub had made for some excitement, but we survived. Willie wasn't up to walking just yet, but he sent me a whistle he'd carved. I suppose all had been forgiven.

We followed the south bank of the North Platte for a way. Just before turning southward, we spotted another wagon train following the Oregon Trail. As we waved greetings, I found myself wondering how many more such caravans would be passing through before the great wave of westward migration slacked off.

Chapter 6

New Trouble Unfolds

Mukue held his head high as he took in the cool, crystal-clear air of the prairie. He felt right good under my saddle. September had arrived, and it sure felt great to be healthy enough to work the ranch again. We'd expanded our acreage, so there was plenty of riding to be done by way of ensuring that all was well. We only had about three dozen head of cattle to look after, as we raised them for our own sustenance. Importantly, they kept me mindful of their dispositions and quirks such that I wouldn't lose my cowboying touch when we got our Texas ranch operational.

As I absentmindedly stroked my new bear claw necklace, I took in the wondrous vista that lay before me. Rolling grass-covered prairie broken with deep crevices and stands of cottonwood and distant lodgepole pine. A couple of miles to the west stood the Laramie Mountains. Soon enough, they'd be capped with snow. I thought back to my pa telling me how the soldiers from Fort Laramie journeyed the sixty miles to obtain wood for constructing the fort. Many a soldier lost his life to the harassment of Lakota warriors. What a high price to have paid.

Mukue reared back from a rattler. Dang, but those slithery varmints were abundant. I found myself looking forward to colder weather and critters hibernating. Perhaps one of the advantages of riding a formerly wild mustang stallion was that he was used to avoiding rattlesnakes. I imagined Mukue had experienced his share of protecting his mares from predators.

Taabe ran along with us this day. He'd soon be growing out his winter coat. The rattlers never seemed to bother him. Whatever God's message in sending him to me, I was in no position to doubt the Lord's wisdom.

I thought back on our visit with Guernsey a few days back. It had gone quite well. In fact, we'd likely have enjoyed his hospitality longer had I not felt compelled to return home. We had a breeding operation to run. I also reckoned to investigate the Wyoming Stock Growers Association down in Cheyenne. While we concentrated on breeding horses and weren't raising cattle for market, I had it figured that the association would connect me with many cattlemen who'd need well-bred Quarter Horses. Lingering in my mind was whether the members would be prejudiced against my ancestry. I was determined to try. There were old codgers like Willie who held deep-rooted hatred for folks of skin colors other than their own. I hoped that the members of the association just might be above such intolerance.

The Laramie Cross Breed Ranch seemed to be running well. Cutter and Moon, our new hands, seemed to be working out well. They sure enough were handy while I'd gone to Texas and then during my recuperation. Cutter was a lanky, rangy sort of fellow carrying just enough weight to hold his own against a stiff breeze.

When he talked, he'd usually twist the ends of his mustache with rope-worn fingers. He knew horses like he knew the back of his hand. Moon was a bigger man, though shorter than me. He'd been a cavalry trooper, so he fully appreciated the care of horses. Anyway, my erstwhile partner and foreman, Chester Donovan, appeared to have picked solid men.

The brief journey with Morning Star to visit Guernsey had to some degree mimicked our times traveling across Wyoming before the ranch and children. We'd been on the run from the rogue Cheyenne warrior Bull Elk. This left me wondering what had become of Wally Wallace, the aging mountain man who'd befriended us and showed up at our times of peril. I found myself yearning for us to travel the wild frontier again, though it would never be the same frontier. Time and humans were changing the landscape even as I thought on it. There'd be protected havens out of man's reach, but ranches, farms, forts, railroads, and towns were carving up the frontier.

I suppose I was becoming quite the philosopher. I'd begun to read Locke's *Two Treatises of Government*, so that may have accounted for my present interest in the world around me. It struck me how Locke's thinking was a foundation for the United States. He was a proponent of natural rights protected by a government that was limited and existed by the consent of the people. I found it especially enlightening that a government that fails to protect its citizens' natural rights loses its legitimacy. Locke wrote that the people held the right to overthrow a government that became tyrannical and violated the established social contract. This caused me to reflect on the constant forging and breaking of treaties between the White man and Red man. From what I could tell, the treaty was simply a tool to forestall the inevitable, all-swallowing wave of settlement.

There I was, daydreaming about things far bigger than me, when I noticed a trio of riders following the south bank of the Laramie River about a mile off. I was atop a bluff overlooking the distant river. As I scanned the river a half mile or so ahead of them, I saw a herd of elk wade across. Beyond them, some grizzlies were busily catching fish along the shore. I couldn't make out much about the men, as they were too far off to make out much. A packhorse trailed them, so they likely weren't out on a brief jaunt across the country-side. They were beyond the southern border of my property, but I found myself curious as to what they were up to. If they stayed their present course, they'd reach Fort Laramie in a few hours. Even at a distance, I could see that they were a bit unsteady in their saddles. I chuckled to myself, as they must have been liquored up.

I shrugged and mounted up. I was about to turn Mukue north and head home when I saw the riders pull up. One dismounted, pulled a rifle, and shot an elk. I reckoned there was nothing special there. It was late afternoon, and the men were likely hungry. The very thought of elk steak made my mouth water a little. As I nudged Mukue forward, my eyes caught the men bringing down a second elk and then a third. About the time they wounded a fourth elk, I'd headed Mukue toward them.

* * *

I headed toward the killing field at a full gallop. My head swam with the indignation of men killing for the sake of killing. It brought back visions of prairies littered with buffalo carcasses.

Two more rifle shots rent the air as I closed the distance to the three men. I'd closed to within a couple of hundred yards when I had to pull up. The men had dismounted, leaving their mounts and packhorse unattended. While the men were focused on their savagery, three grizzlies approached from behind them. Why were the grizzlies attracted to them? Or was it the dead elk? The horses? They didn't normally attack humans or their horses. The scene appeared chaotic at first until I realized that one of the bears was limping. Had they shot a bear, too?

What was going on? The first of the grizzlies took a swipe at a horse. The cayuse's scream got the attention of the three men. They turned and began firing wildly toward the attacking bears. What on God's earth had possessed them? It came to me that the men were totally drunk. Was there any hope of saving them from the fix they'd put themselves in, plus preserving the lives of elk and bears? At least, the elk had begun to stampede off by way of escaping the guns. The bears? They meant business, especially the wounded one.

I dismounted and drew my Spencer from the saddle scabbard. I hoped that by stopping the wounded grizzly, the others would run off before they too were wounded. Fortunately, the men were so frantic that their aim was terrible. One horse was down. I took careful aim at the big grizzly and squeezed the trigger. I caught him in the head. It stopped him. As his paw swiped at the wound, I put a second round into his chest. That finished him. The men had run out of ammunition by now, yet kept trying to shoot. They were too drunk to reload. The other two bears apparently figured they'd had enough and ran off.

By now, the men had begun to realize that someone other than them had killed the bear.

I mounted Mukue and rode in slowly. As yet, the men hadn't the sense to reload, but I wasn't taking any chances. One had even passed out. I rode closer, keeping my Spencer pointed in their general direction. In their drunken condition, I didn't figure to trust them. "Drop your guns!" I hollered as I waded Mukue across the Laramie.

The men looked at me through rheumy eyes and gaping mouths. From what I could tell, they hadn't yet realized that it was me who'd saved their lives.

With my hair braided and clothed in fringed buckskins, I suppose I resembled an Indian warrior to their unschooled eyes. "Drop your guns," I repeated.

Blank looks.

I pulled my Bowie knife. "Drop those guns, or I'll scalp you where you stand," I growled.

That got their attention. They dropped their rifles and stood tottering helplessly beside the bear's carcass.

I sheathed my knife and approached to within about twenty feet. From what I could tell, the men were useless so far as doing what I had in mind. What was that? I aimed to see the elk and bear field dressed and skinned, and as much meat as we could load packed off to Fort Laramie. I dismounted and collected the rifles and two revolvers. The man who'd passed out had no sidearm. "Sit!" I ordered.

They dutifully followed my command. I might have begun to find this a tad humorous were the scene not so serious. I remained cautious. The men's condition bordered on helpless, but there was no telling what they were capable of.

I checked their saddlebags and the packhorse, emptying what little remained of their whiskey supply. One of the men raised his hand in weak protest, and I managed to control the urge to bust him up the side of his head. They'd needlessly killed elk and the bear, which served to rile me no end.

"Who you be?" croaked one of the men.

"The man who saved your worthless lives," I replied as I poured out the last few drops of booze. With that, I lifted the passed-out man by the collar and dragged him into the chilled waters of the Laramie. He quickly awoke, blubbering and spitting river water. I laid his sputtering body back on the riverbank and went for the second man. He offered no resistance as I gave him a dunking aimed at sobering him. The third man, likely fearing the knife at my waist and wanting to keep his hair, crawled into the river without my assistance. Finally, I had them sprawled out before me and beginning to dry out. With a little luck, I hoped to have them sober enough to go to work field dressing the elk and bear while still getting to Fort Laramie before dark.

* * *

Oh my, but we managed to pack away the meat from two of the four elk. The bears and a collection of scavengers got to them before I could rally the three ne'er-do-wells to the tasks at hand. At least a few critters would be well fed this day. I skinned the bear; a job I had some all-too-recent experience with.

The poor packhorse handled most of the load. Of course, I made the men dump all but the most essential gear they'd carried so as to make room for the meat cuts and bear skin. I escorted the little caravan to Fort Laramie, with me riding at the rear with Spencer carbine in hand, just in case any of the miscreants got frisky.

The pre-dusk shadows had grown long as the fort came into view. The men had remained silent during our brief journey. They just endured the ride as best they could while nursing booze-addled heads.

The expressions of the guards at the Fort Laramie entrance were priceless as they waved me through. Their mirth was justified, as I'd made the three men shed their boots and pants to lighten the burdens on their horses.

This time, Taabe followed along into the fort, much to the amazement of the soldiers.

A corporal led us to Captain Hayes' headquarters. Someone must have gotten the word to Hayes ahead of us, because he stood out front, awaiting our arrival. He dismissed the corporal with a quick salute and came forward to me with two of his lieutenants. "Greetings, Mr. O'Toole," exclaimed Hayes with a respectful salute.

"My pleasure, Captain. I've brought some elk for your men," said I calmly with a salute of my own.

"And these three?" he asked.

"I believe you call them poachers, Captain. They killed some elk and a bear for the fun of it. I do believe they're well along to learning a lesson. The bear was one of three that attacked them. I shot and killed one, and the other two ran off. These men were so drunk that they tried to fire empty rifles." It was all I could do to keep a straight face at the recall of the frantic efforts of the men to shoot the bear without bullets. "I am pleased to leave them to your company, sir."

"We're grateful for the elk meat, Isa. We'll be pleased to relieve you of these men." With that, a half dozen soldiers appeared and escorted the poachers to the guard house. "I'm not sure what our code says about dealing with civilian lawbreakers, but we'll come up with something," he added.

"Is the major in, sir?" I asked.

Hayes gave me a curious look.

"I reckoned this here bearskin might look good in his quarters, Captain. It's a thank you for saving my arm. Sorry I don't have another bear for you, sir."

"That's right thoughtful of you," replied Hayes. "He's away for a couple of days, but I'll see that he gets your gift. Meanwhile, you're welcome to bunk here with us tonight."

"I appreciate your hospitality, Captain, but there's a full moon to light the way and my family will be expecting me."

We saluted, and I headed Mukue for home. My heart was full with the satisfaction of having saved many elk and, hopefully, taught three men a valuable lesson. The Lord had surely protected me.

* * *

I expect that I could thank Taabe for my ride from Fort Laramie being uneventful. We heard occasional owl hoots, coyote howls, and cricket serenades, but nothing to fear. Taabe led the way home and was ever alert to danger. The full moon and millions of stars were the next best thing to daylight. It was hard to believe that just a handful of years back, I'd have been on the lookout for hostile Indians. That danger was pretty much gone. Some feared that Sitting Bull's return would incite a resurgence of fighting, but I wasn't among them. Other than ongoing squabbles with Apache in the southern reaches of Texas and the Arizona Territory, the tribes would fight no more.

The lights of the night can be tricky. Trees and shrubs can seem like ghostly apparitions in the soft whiteness of moonbeams. Shadows are barely perceptible. I was thankful to be astride a cayuse with experience roaming the prairies and valleys of Wyoming. Mukue knew the ground well. As to predators, if any were lurking, they'd surely have decided we weren't tempting enough to risk attacking. The air had grown chilly; a sure harbinger of the seasons to come. By the end of September, we'd likely see the first snowfall.

As we approached Laramie Cross Breed Ranch, the welcoming glow of candles shone in the windows of our home. We rode up to the stable in the middle of the night with nary a soul in sight. After settling Mukue in his stall, I quietly headed to our front door. I'd barely touched the doorlatch when it swung open. Morning Star peeked around the edge of the door. The soft candlelight and warmth of the hearth behind her cast off the chill of the night. Hugging her warmed me even more.

"You took long," said Morning Star softly.

"Bit of a dust up on the south range with some drunken poachers. I escorted them to Fort Laramie." That just about summed up my day.

"You could have stayed at the fort. Much danger at night," she observed.

I smiled gently as I held her in my arms. "I wanted to be at home with you."

She kicked the door shut behind us and led me to the bearskin on the floor in front of the hearth.

* * *

"Are you going to Cheyenne?" asked Morning Star as she placed a plate teeming with eggs, biscuits, and venison sausage before me.

I paused my fork. "I'm thinking it can wait until spring. From what our friend Guernsey said, the folks I'd be talking with are just beginning their ranch operations. I suppose that I could visit a ranch or two, but..."

"But?" she pressed.

"I've been thinking about Guernsey's comment that these eastern folks think highly of themselves and very likely hold prejudices against Indians. Instead of asking to join their Cheyenne Club, I'd rather they ask me to join. If they don't, I can still sell them fine Quarter Horses." I was of a mind to avoid enduring rejection based upon my ancestry.

Morning Star nodded. "Must face *niya*."

Face ghosts? I knew she was right. However, the ghost of prejudice was all too real, and I saw no benefit to crossing the bridge over that divide. If the issue came up, I'd deal with it. I saw no point in proactively confronting folks over my heritage. I'd done a bit of praying over this and felt that God was telling me to not press the issue. It was a matter of having the strength of spirit to be above the contrived cultural grievances of others. My Comanche ancestors had dealt in killing and slavery, but I was two generations separated from those people. I didn't believe that I should be punished for the sins of my ancestors. It would be akin to punishing White men today for the slave owners of the past. "I see no *niya*, Awentia," I responded.

She smiled. "Isa strong *sunipu*."

Indeed, my medicine was strong. I took a bite of sausage and smiled as I realized we were mixing hints of the Lakota and Comanche languages in our everyday speech. Our cultures were mixed. I wished that could be the way of the world. "I'll take a ride south and get acquainted."

It was only a couple of days' ride, and I reckoned it wouldn't hurt to meet a couple of these would-be cattlemen. I doubted they'd ever mucked a stall, but I wouldn't hold that against them. It occurred to me that meeting the cowhands who would actually operate their ranches made the best sense. They'd be the ones demanding fine horse stock and appreciating all it took to produce top Quarter Horses.

"Donovan has news," offered Morning Star.

"News?" I replied.

"Pearl with child," she informed me.

I savored a sip of coffee and dipped a biscuit in melted butter. "Chester will make a good father." I gazed into Morning Star's eyes. Was our third child on its way?

As if reading my mind, she shook her head. Moses and Michael were plenty for now.

"Speaking of Donovan, I understand that we have a dozen two-year-olds ready for sale. Maybe I should take a half dozen with me to Cheyenne," I reckoned by way of speculative thinking. It seemed to make sense to show off our Quarter Horses to cowboys hanging around the place. There would be several cattle drives finishing up, and the corrals near the railhead would be teeming with cowhands. With the Wyoming winter ahead, they'd either settle down for the winter or high-tail it back south.

"Make sense. Cowboys have chance to know horse before next trail drive." Morning Star was certainly learning the whys and wherefores of the horse business.

The demand was waiting for us. We simply had to fill the supply. Of course, we were still a long way from satisfying the horseflesh needs of hundreds of cowpokes. As I'd learned, the good news would be that limited supply and high demand drove up prices. We could earn a handsome profit on a half dozen prize Quarter Horses. I still had those sacks of gold hidden away, so the profit would serve to pay our ranch hands and cover most operating expenses. The future was looking right fine.

Chapter 7

The Association

I thought back a tad on my conversation with Guernsey about Cheyenne. Guernsey had shared with me that the brothers Hubert and Arthur Teschemacher and a fellow named Frederick Ogden de Billier had come to Cheyenne and were aiming to set up an outfit called the Teschemacher & de Billier Cattle Company. They were planning to buy up smaller ranches and set up a spread that could turn out thousands of head to ship to market by rail from Cheyenne. Of course, my thinking was that raising beeves required cowboys, and cowboys needed horses. They craved Quarter Horses, and why shouldn't I be their supplier?

As I understood it, according to Guernsey's description, these were men used to the refined culture of wealthy Harvard University graduates. While Hubert figured to be active in their ranching operations, Arthur was a stockholder and would be an onlooker, enjoying the spoils of what they hoped would be a profitable business venture.

Being of the sort that they were, the Teschemacher

brothers sought an outlet for interests more suitable to the lives of privilege they'd enjoyed back east. According to Guernsey, they teamed with Charles and Henry Oelkrich, William and Thomas Sturgis, and Richard and Moreton Frewen to found the Cheyenne Club. Originally founded as the Cactus Club, the fine edifice their money built included second-floor apartments for members and guests. First-floor facilities included a world-class dining room with a chef imported from Canada, a billiard room, card rooms, a reading room, and a lounge for drinking and smoking. Strict rules forbid profanity, drunkenness, fighting, card cheating, pipe smoking, and betting. Violators were summarily expelled forever.

Were these my kind of people? Likely as not. I was hardly from an exclusive monied class. Those of us who'd grown up ranching in Wyoming worked hard for every dollar. The grit under our fingernails and the odor of livestock permeating our skin gave testament to our hard-won successes.

As I'd discussed with Morning Star, I reckoned to head to check out some of the spreads around Cheyenne and learn what I could about their exclusive club. It would also afford me the opportunity to look into the Wyoming Stock Growers Association. I might have a better chance of joining the association than gaining membership to the Cheyenne Club. However, I sensed that the two organizations were inextricably linked by blood. Guernsey had advised that the association was run by club members.

We decided to leave Joe Moon to watch over the ranch while Donovan and Cutter accompanied me to Cheyenne. Having a couple of hands to help with the horses would make the journey much easier than if I'd tried to herd the critters myself.

* * *

We were a right handsome trio heading south with a packhorse and six fine Quarter Horses. With autumn in the air and its accompanying uncertain weather, we reckoned to spend no more than three days around Cheyenne before heading home. Taabe followed along for a while, but disappeared as we got closer to Cheyenne.

By my reckoning, we were about twenty miles from Cheyenne when we encountered our first cowhands. They were apparently scouting for prime grazing land. After the usual greetings, we sat a spell to discuss goings on around the cattle town. They confirmed the creation of the Cheyenne Club and how their bosses made nice with the Wyoming Stock Growers Association.

Finally, one of the men got up and began looking more closely at our Quarter Horses. He addressed Donovan, likely figuring me, the half-breed, was just a hand. "Y'all have some fine hosses," he observed. "They fer sale?"

I figured the men were likely sitting on their wages from a cattle drive, but what they had in their pockets wouldn't be enough to buy one of our stock. However, the outfit they worked for surely could.

Donovan smiled at the cowboy. "Y'all will have to ask the boss," he said with a thumb toward me.

"They're for sale," I said, striving to appear unbothered by the slight.

"We don't deal with Injuns," cracked the cowboy.

"Wait, Slim," offered one of his companions. "Them's

right fine horses. Don't matter none to me who be sellin' them."

"Shut yer pie hole, kid," retorted Slim.

The kid wasn't to be deterred. "Yer just actin' up because yuh ain't got enough money for such fine hosses."

Slim threw the kid a nasty look. "I got money," he boasted. "How much fer the grey?" Once again, he directed his question at Donovan.

"How much do you have?" I was becoming irritated by the man's obvious prejudice.

"Told yuh, I don't deal with no scalp takers," insisted Slim.

"We'll be moving on," I said and nodded to Donovan and Cutter to begin urging our Quarter Horses along.

With that, Slim drew his revolver. It wasn't a fast move, and he was lucky that it wasn't. He found himself staring down the muzzle of my Spencer from a mere twenty feet away. He slid the gun back into its holster. "We ain't done with yuh," he growled. He turned to head off, but his two companions held back.

"My name's Billy. How much?" asked the kid.

I was well aware of what a drover earned on a cattle drive, and it was nowhere near the amount necessary to purchase one of my horses. "I'm Isa O'Toole. I own the Laramie Cross Breed Ranch up on the North Platte River. My ranch hands are Chester Donovan and Will Cutter." Introductions completed, I laid the hard truth before Billy. "My horses went for two hundred eighty-five dollars each two years back in Cheyenne. Can you come anywhere close to that?"

Disappointment swept across Billy's face. "Got a hunnert," he said meekly.

I shook my head. As a man of faith, I had compassion

for those of lesser means, but I was in the business of selling top-of-the-line Quarter Horses and had ranch hands who counted on being paid. "Who's your boss, Billy?"

"I work fer the JA Ranch," he replied. "Mr. Goodnight be my boss."

I'd heard of the JA Ranch from the two bushwhackers whom I dealt with back in the summer after my nearly disastrous trip to Texas. The JA folks owned most of Palo Duro Canyon. This Goodnight fellow, Charles Goodnight to be exact, was partnered with John Adair to run the JA Ranch and drive cattle to the eastern markets on the Union Pacific Railroad out of Cheyenne. "How about you introduce me to Mr. Goodnight. Maybe we can work something out with that grey stallion."

Billy nodded enthusiastically. "An' I don't think he feel the way Slim does," he added apologetically.

* * *

I expected the upside of meeting Goodnight would be the possible sale of our horses, but the downside could be whether he had ties to the Wyoming Stock Growers Association. I was eager to show and hopefully sell my horses to an association member. Nevertheless, far be it from me to deprive the JA Ranch of my fine Quarter Horses.

Billy's other companion had gone on with Slim, so he led the way to where Goodnight was holed up before heading back to Texas. Along the way, we got better acquainted. Billy even shared a little-known fact. It seemed that the famed rancher Charles Goodnight had an aversion to sleeping indoors. He loved the sense of freedom carried on the night air. He had built an earthen and log dugout on the JA Ranch, though Billy said he had plans to build a fine two-story home for his wife. I reckoned that his love of the outdoors would surely endear him to me.

Billy led us right into the city and to a tent pitched behind the Inter-Ocean Hotel, the finest such establishment in Cheyenne. A man was standing beside the tent reading papers while there was still daylight.

Billy dismounted and walked toward Goodnight with hat in hand. "Pardon, Mr. Goodnight, sir. I done brought some folks fer yuh to meet."

Goodnight looked at Billy, then turned to glance up at us still aboard our horses. "Who might you fellas be and where are you from?" he asked.

"I'm Isa O'Toole, sir. I own the Laramie Cross Breed Ranch up north. We cross Quarter Horses with mustangs to breed fine horses for cattlemen." I swept my hand toward the six horses we'd brought with us.

Goodnight took a long look at our Quarter Horses. He smiled. "To tell the truth, Mr. O'Toole, I like that bay you're sitting upon." He gave Mukue an admiring once-over. "Looks like a one-man bronc," he added.

"Your hand Billy here thought you might be interested in fine Quarter Horses, Mr. Goodnight." I was already pleased that Goodnight was talking with me rather than Donovan and Cutter. "Billy is especially partial to yonder grey stallion."

Goodnight took a side glance toward Billy and nodded. "Billy's been a right fine drover," remarked Goodnight. He strolled over to our little remuda and began examining the grey while we dismounted.

"You like this one, Billy?" asked Goodnight.

Billy nodded with barely controlled excitement. "Yessir, boss. Only, I ain't got enough money."

Goodnight turned to me. "You have family in Texas, Mr. O'Toole?"

"My pa owns a ranch north of Bandera, and my own spread lies nearby." By this time, I had it figured that Goodnight was likely flush with cash from selling a couple of thousand head of prime beeves.

"Jack O'Toole? Why, we had some of his stock join our drive last year." Goodnight rubbed his chin thoughtfully and finally settled his gaze on Billy. "I'll give you a hundred seventy-five for the grey long as Billy contributes another seventy-five. It'll be his to ride and pay me back to own him full." He smiled at the pleasure on Billy's face. "And, Mr. O'Toole, I'd sure like that chestnut stallion. Will you take three hundred for him?"

Donovan was already stepping forward with the bills of sale for the two Quarter Horses, and we consummated the deal.

"One question, if you don't mind, Mr. Goodnight," I ventured.

"How's that?" he responded.

"Are you acquainted with the Cheyenne Club and the Wyoming Stock Growers Association?" It was a bold question.

Goodnight chuckled. "I come to Cheyenne to sell my beeves. They board a Union Pacific train to the Chicago meatpackers. I don't have time for a bunch of rich dandies trying to imitate their exclusive eastern clubs. As to the association, I expect it to be right good for Wyoming ranchers, but it's run by those Cheyenne Club fellows. And the local newspapers? Why, those easterners control the editorial content of the *Cheyenne Daily Sun* and *Cheyenne Daily Leader*. Those news folks hold considerable sway over Cheyenne and beyond, but they answer to the money. If you're asking whether you should get involved, I'd advise staying clear. Sell them your horses, but you don't need them otherwise. Matter of fact, I'm thinking of establishing a cattleman association down on the Texas Panhandle. There'll be no fancy carryings on."

The influence over the newspapers, even if only perceived, was concerning. By my way of thinking, newspapers should be a bastion for free speech. After all, to embrace a God-breathed view of man places free speech on the side of the angels. Blasphemies can't hurt where faith is strong, but killing free speech by the evil influences of mankind is as a death knell. Survival needs a full grasp of freedom's value, while faith defeats the evil rulers and unseen powers and engages the foe in the battle to win. For when speech is free, freedom flowers. I'd read enough of John Locke already to realize the influence of the voices of the people. The newspapers were part of those voices, but with considerable reach. The influence of the Cheyenne Club members was deeply concerning.

I was wary of folks who dabbled in power and control. Too much influence is known to take folks where they have no business being. It tends to breed evil. Worse, that evil is often disguised as good. If we accept evil masked as good, it begs the question of whether that deprives us of what is best? While the wealthy men at the Cheyenne Club were welcome to their choices, it left me wondering what undergirded the intentions of those who wielded the power afforded by money and societal station.

As I had come to see it, men pursued pleasures and accumulated possessions. As they gained popularity, they would seek prestige and eventually the power that led to control. Shucks, if I were only a half-breed rancher figuring this out, I had to wonder whether anyone else was onto this game? "It's been a pleasure, Mr. Goodnight. We must be getting on. I reckon to show my Quarter Horses to folks down at the stockyards."

"You head to Texas again, son, you be sure to stop by the JA," he invited.

* * *

"Mr. Goodnight has a right low opinion of them Cheyenne Club folks," observed Donovan once we were down the trail a bit.

I nodded. "I expect that's good advice, Chester."

We now had our remaining four Quarter Horses on halters with tethers to better control them as we approached the seeming chaos of the stockyards. Between bawling cattle, neighing horses, and shouting cowboys, there was a lot of distraction. We rode straight up the main street, passing the Cheyenne Club on the way. I had to admit that it was impressive.

As we drew close, a man stepped into the street and hailed us. "Howdy, gents. You lookin' to sell them fine lookin' hosses?" The man was big, likely nearly as tall as me and perhaps twenty pounds heavier. I judged him to be pushing forty or so years. He had an aura of importance about him.

I nodded and smiled from my perch atop Mukue. "Could be, sir. Who's asking?"

"Name's Wynn Dixon. I'm foreman of one of the Teschemacher spreads," he replied. He looked around a bit furtively as though hoping to make an exclusive deal for my horses. "You're from north of here, aren't you?"

I nodded. He seemed to know a little about me. I supposed my reputation must have been catching hold.

"Name's Isa O'Toole. These fine Quarter Horses have been bred with mustangs to enhance their performance."

"Heard 'bout that." Dixon had already begun a closer inspection of our stock. "That's a handsome mustang you're riding," he observed. He took a step toward Mukue, but my fine stallion gave him a nip that told him to keep his distance. "One-man horse?"

"Pretty much," I replied with a laugh. "He found me and doesn't cotton to any other man."

"I like your stock, Mr. O'Toole. Mr. Teschemacher gives me free rein to improve our operations, and I'd say your Quarter Horses would be a fine addition. I assume they're saddle-broke?"

"They're saddle-broke and ready for some cowboys to get better acquainted," I responded.

"You take two fifty apiece?" asked Dixon.

I glanced at Donovan and Cutter and shook my head. "Why, Mr. Dixon, these are right fine Quarter Horses. Your hands could be riding the best horseflesh within a thousand miles." The thousand miles was an exaggeration, but it got my point across. "I sold two this morning for better than your offer." I purposely didn't reply with a price.

"Hear tell you done some Indian fighting and scouted for Colonel Stanley up on the Yellowstone. Now you have your own spread. I bet y'all could use the money from selling as many horses as you can." Dixon rubbed his chin as though deep in thought. "How about two hundred seventy-five?" he finally offered.

"I sold Quarter Horses here in Cheyenne a couple of years back at that price," I noted. I waved my hand at the bustling city and stockyards. "Demand sure has increased." I had a price in mind, and Dixon wasn't there yet. "Your boss runs with those Cheyenne Club folks, doesn't he?" My implication was that he had a lot more money-resources to draw upon.

Dixon smiled. "Final offer is three twenty," he declared with a set jaw.

I looked over at Donovan.

He gave an imperceptible nod.

I wasn't seeking his approval, but I wanted to be sure my hands didn't think I was being cheated. "Mr. Dixon, you have a deal."

Donovan brought the horses forward, along with the bills of sale specifying the particulars of each horse.

Dixon motioned to a couple of his cowhands, then turned to me. "Let's mosey on down to the bank, Mr. O'Toole. I don't carry that sort of money on me."

I dismounted, and we shook hands.

"Where'd you come up with those bear claws?" he asked, as we headed toward the bank.

"The usual way," I replied.

He gave me a curious look.

"Had a squabble with a bear and decided he didn't look so good wearing a fingernail necklace."

Dixon appreciated my sense of humor. "I heard you were tough," he said with a grin. "You ever look to wrangle cattle, come see me."

"Actually, I own a spread in Texas. Been working with cattle and horses most of my life," I shared. "The Lord's been right good to me."

"I expect I should introduce you to Mr. Teschemacher," Dixon suggested as we entered the bank.

I caught his inference. Despite my buckskins and Comanche ancestry, my owning multiple ranches apparently qualified me for attention from the monied elite of Cheyenne. "I'd be up for that, Mr. Dixon," I said with feigned modesty. "However, we'll be heading north tomorrow morning, and I'd prefer to meet your boss when I have time to relax and linger a bit here in Cheyenne." I didn't feel a need to tell of my business with Goodnight and certainly not the advice of him and Guernsey.

"Perhaps in the spring," responded Dixon as we stood beside the teller window at the First National Bank. He soon handed me thirteen hundred dollars in gold coins in a heavy leather sack.

The heavy sack caused me to realize that I needed to open a bank account, as carrying around so much cash was not a good idea. Even giving Donovan his share and paying Cutter and Moon would leave me with more than I cared to carry on the trail home. "I've got some business to tend to here, Mr. Dixon. It's been a pleasure."

We shook hands, and Dixon departed. I turned to the bank teller. "I'm Isa O'Toole, and I'd like to set up an account," I informed him.

"Let me get Mr. Sparks," said the teller in his suit and tie as he looked down his long nose at my trail-worn buckskins. He'd been staring judgmentally at me during the earlier transaction with Dixon.

A few moments later, Sparks emerged from a private office. He gave me an appraising once-over and rolled his eyes. "We don't do business with Indians," he said offhandedly.

"I'm half White," I informed him resolutely. I then made just enough motion with the sack to cause the coins to jingle just a bit. If he had a problem with my heritage, I figured an appeal to greed might influence him. "I wonder what Mr. Teschemacher would think of you refusing me." I wasn't overjoyed at having to invoke the name of a person I had yet to meet, but figured it was worth the effort. "His foreman just bought four of my

Quarter Horses, and I reckon to park my money some-place safe."

Sparks glanced nervously at the teller. I could tell that his mouth was going a bit dry.

"What will it be, Mr. Sparks?" I started to turn toward the door.

"Er…let me see what I can do," he said disconcertedly. He looked about the lobby, but to his apparent relief, there were no patrons. "Please…follow me." Sparks led me to his office.

I wasn't certain whether to be annoyed or amused by Sparks' behavior. There weren't a lot of banks in Wyoming, so choices were limited, and the Cheyenne location was about as convenient as any.

Despite the awkward start, we did get an account established for the Laramie Cross Breed Ranch. By way of good business sense, I made certain that Morning Star had access as well as Donovan. As to Mr. Sparks, he offered no further trouble despite his prejudice. Playing to the banker's greed had been the lever needed to get him past his personal foibles.

* * *

Donovan, Cutter, and I spent the night camping not far from Goodnight's spot behind the Inter-Ocean Hotel. I did treat the boys to a fine steak dinner at the hotel.

I was setting beside my bedroll, preparing to catch some much-needed shuteye, when sounds other than crickets caught my ears. In the dim moonlight and the light shed from the windows of the hotel, I heard giggling and the soft swishing of cloth.

Donovan was already fast asleep, but I saw Cutter sit

up and take notice. The young man was barely eighteen years old and not yet experienced with women.

It seems that a couple of young ladies from the saloon up the street were looking for some fun with other than the sweaty, drunken sots who comprised their normal trade. They found Cutter and laughed flirtatiously toward me.

"Hi, boys. Y'all wanna have some good times?" they asked coquettishly, baring more skin than I was comfortable with.

Cutter and I exchanged looks. I shook my head, though I couldn't condemn Cutter were he to succumb to the women's charms. Neither was I going to encourage him to avail himself of their invitation. I was no nursemaid, and it wasn't uncommon for cowboys to satisfy themselves with liquor and women.

The girls were all atwitter around Cutter. He looked at me for help, but I shrugged and hunkered down in my bedroll.

I spent the next couple of hours serenaded by noises from Cutter and the young ladies.

* * *

At first light, we were on the trail back to the ranch. I could have used a bit more sleep, but I reckoned to catch up the next night. Our little trip to Cheyenne had pretty much met or even exceeded expectations. We'd sold all of the Quarter Horses for nearly two thousand dollars total and made connections that I fully anticipated to be invaluable in the future. Come spring, I'd seek out Teschemacher, and if we rode down to Texas, I'd visit the JA Ranch. There was nothing to complain about, not even the couple of instances of prejudice I'd dealt with.

After paying Donovan and Cutter, plus setting aside wages for Moon, most of the money from the sale of the Quarter Horses remained in the First National Bank. With greater than a two-day ride ahead of us, it seemed a blessing to not be carrying a passel of gold coins with us. If by some chance we were waylaid, our financial losses wouldn't be so great. Additionally, the money in the bank would be earning interest. Despite his dogmatic bigotry, Mr. Sparks had given me a cursory lesson in compound interest, the amount the bank paid me for the privilege of holding my money. Upon reflection, it seemed to me that the bank's interest was a paltry sum compared to the greater though riskier returns on investing in land. I did find myself much preferring the methods that Adair, Goodnight, King, and my pa used down in Texas to build their ranching businesses as compared to the likes of the members of the Cheyenne Club.

CHAPTER 8

MIXED BLESSINGS

We arrived home a little after midday. The first week of October was upon us, and we'd been dusted with the first snow flurries the night before. Cutter and I never talked about his fling with the soiled doves, and we'd resisted teasing him about it. What was done was done. Donovan mentioned that he'd been aware of the ranch hand's carrying on but ignored it. Like me, he was happy to be home with his wife. Pearl was expected to give birth any day.

I curried Mukue and let him loose in the corral. After having been away for a few days, he was casting his eyes toward the Quarter Horse mares in an adjoining corral. I watched him for a couple of minutes, then headed for our front door. Leaning against the cabin wall beside the door were a massive set of elk antlers. They'd been cut away, not shed. I smiled. Morning Star was ever the huntress.

The door latch flipped, and I pushed through to see Morning Star beading a buckskin dress. "Isa!" she said excitedly and ran to my arms. By that, I gathered that she was ever happy to see me.

We hugged and kissed, then I stepped back. "You've been hunting?" I asked with a nod toward the antlers at the front door.

She broke free and headed for the coffee pot. "Sit, husband. Awentia tell," she said with a smile, as she poured my coffee and some for herself.

I anticipated some story about going hunting, though I figured Moon would have mentioned that sort of thing when I was in the stable tending to Mukue. I took a sip of hot coffee and was ready for a story.

"Big elk," she began with arms outstretched. Then she laughed. She simply couldn't go through with a made-up story. "While Isa away, bull elk come too close to corrals. Awentia walk out to feed horses, See elk. He upwind and not see me." She sat opposite me, holding the coffee cup in both hands. "I take rifle and shoot elk. One bullet," she added proudly.

She had grabbed the rifle that was always setting just inside the door and quickly dispatched the elk bull. I was impressed but not surprised at her only needing a single shot. We'd be eating especially well for a few days. "Is good. Where's the hide?"

"Awentia tanning hide in barn. Meat in cold cellar. Make sausage, too."

She'd done it all. I looked across the table, momentarily transfixed by my Lakota wife.

She blushed, then turned the conversation to me. "Isa sell horses?"

"Yes," I replied and went on to describe the events around Cheyenne, especially my meetings with Goodnight and Teschemacher's foreman. She was pleased that

I'd set up an account with the bank. I decided to not tell her about the prejudices I'd encountered or Cutter's dalliance.

"Isa join association?" she asked.

I was pleased that she hadn't forgotten that one of my purposes was to learn what I could about the Wyoming Stock Growers Association and whether it was a suitable fit for Laramie Cross Breed Ranch. "Seems the association is run by the rich folks at the Cheyenne Club. Mr. Goodnight confirmed what Mr. Guernsey advised."

Morning Star took a sip of her coffee and gazed thoughtfully at me. "What of Comanche blood?" she asked tentatively.

"Seems that money and prime Quarter Horses are more important than my ancestors," I replied with a sheepish sort of smile. About this time, I became aware that the aroma of elk stew was permeating the air around us.

She smiled. "Isa hungry?"

"Hungry for Awentia, but the stew will do for now," I responded with a mischievous laugh.

Morning Star arose, skirted the table to brush a kiss across my waiting lips, and went over to the stove to tend to the stew. Moses and Michael appeared as if from nowhere and crawled up onto my lap.

"I thought we might visit George and Running Waters before the snows arrive." I tossed out the idea, as I was of a mind to introduce Cutter to their daughter Esmeralda. I was of a mind that the young man needed to settle down with a good woman before he got himself in trouble.

She began ladling out the stew. "Visit be good," she said, then grinned. "Moses can ride mare."

Her words fell on me like a hammer. I hadn't realized that my oldest son was nearing four years old. Despite his lanky build, he was still too small for a regular saddle. We'd have to shorten the fenders to put the stirrups within reach. I was about to say that I'd fix a saddle for him, but Morning Star anticipated me. She always had a way of doing that.

"Awentia make saddle fit."

"Guess we'll go for a ride after dinner," I said and was about to lift a heaping spoonful of stew to my mouth.

"We bless?" reminded Morning Star.

Properly chided, I offered a quick blessing and shoved that spoonful into my mouth. As I thought on it, spending some time with Moses made great sense. The custom with the Comanche and many other tribes was for young boys to be raised by their mothers until they were eleven or twelve years old. It was a matriarchal society in that respect. The men eventually took over, training them to become hunters and warriors. The White man's ways were different. My sons would need to be self-sufficient at as early an age as possible. "Are you ready to ride?" I asked Moses.

He looked up with excitement written across his face. While he was tall for his age, he'd need every ounce of his strength to handle even a fairly docile horse like the mare.

Thoughts of the Wyoming Stock Growers Association and the Cheyenne Club would be put aside for greater use of my time.

No sooner was dinner finished than Moses darted for the stable. I was barely able to keep up. Donovan, Cutter, and Moon were hanging at the bunkhouse and had good laughs at the scene unfolding before them. I was barely inside the stable when Moses emerged leading the mare and dragging the modified saddle. "Help, pa?" he pleaded.

I had the mare saddled and bridled in no time. "Now, lead her to the corral, son."

He looked to the surrounding prairie with a hopeful look.

"Not yet," I said. "Let's teach you to ride first."

With the shortened fenders, there was no way Moses was climbing into the saddle unassisted. This was a situation I'd be sure to keep in mind before he could venture out on his own.

I brought the mare around to a bench and git him to climb into the saddle from that vantage point. We spent the next hour with me leading the horse around the corral while feeding instructions to Moses. Now and then, I'd let go to allow him to direct the mare. I must say that he caught on fast.

We repeated the lessons the next day. Moses was growing sufficiently confident aboard the mare that I saddled Mukue to take my son for a short ride outside the fenced confines of the corrals. Morning Star was all smiles as she watched us ride past the front door.

It took a few more rides together until I felt he was ready for the ride to the Circled Cross Ranch. It was nearly a day's ride to George's spread, so we'd be spending a night there.

* * *

As winter teased us with occasional snow flurries, I realized that I'd not practiced my skills with bow and arrow. In fact, I'd be hard-pressed to find more than a couple of arrows around our house. My beautifully beaded quiver hung empty on a peg near the hearth.

I was determined to rectify this situation, especially as the bow and arrow was effective for hunting as well as battle. I'd witnessed a Lakota hunter drive an arrow clean through a buffalo. The damage an arrow could do to an enemy could be quite devastating.

I strung my bow and decided it was still worthy. It took quite a bit of arm strength to string a war bow. It was about four feet long. Mine was made of ash, though elm, ironwood, cedar, or hickory were used by some tribes. Given the strong pull required to launch an arrow from a war bow, it was little wonder that the shafts could penetrate deep into animal or human. I'd heard of an enemy shot through and pinned to a tree by an arrow deeply embedded in the tree trunk. The bow could also be a psychological weapon, as if a warrior chose to touch an enemy with the tip of his bow, it meant that the enemy was a coward and not worthy of an arrow. Such a disgraced enemy would be shunned by everyone.

With the bow in good condition, I focused my attention on arrows. Cedar and ash branches were the materials I'd been taught to use in fashioning the shafts. Cedar was especially desirable, since it didn't have to be cured. Morning Star and I journeyed out with the children one afternoon and collected about four dozen branches straight enough to use for arrows. Most were ash branches and would have to be cured. I did this by trimming them and wrapping them in two bundles of about two dozen each with rawhide. We'd built a fire behind the house and hung the bundles over the fire at a sufficient height to cure but not burn. The wrapping kept them from warping or bending. It took many days to season the shafts. I took my time gathering materials we'd need when the shafts were ready. Once cured, I scraped the bark off to reveal the yellowish-colored wood beneath.

I cut our arrows to a length of precisely two feet. Notably, tribes could often be identified in part by the length of their arrows. Consistency was important mostly for the sake of accuracy. Once the shafts were trimmed, I cut a notch exactly in the center of the end of each. I then tapered the shaft slightly toward the notch and rounded the end. My next task was quite practical. I carved a zig-zag notch along the shaft. Gross as it may sound, this was to allow blood to escape from whatever wound the arrow made.

The arrowhead came next. Warriors used to make them from natural materials that would hold a sharp edge, like obsidian or flint, but steel arrowheads had become easily available and offered consistency of shape and size. I inserted the arrowheads exactly in the center of the ends of the shafts. I used deer sinew to hold the arrowheads in place, though buffalo or elk would do.

Feathers at the notched end of the arrow came next. The feather was important toward keeping the arrow true to the target. Morning Star had prepared plenty, as I'd chosen to attach three feathers to each arrow. The larger end of each feather was fastened toward the notch and glued in place.

The decorations on arrows identified the warrior. In the case of our arrows, we decided to attach cuttings of hair from our horses. We reckoned that it was rather appropriate for a horse breeding ranch. A couple of bands of red paint completed our supply of arrows.

Naturally, we decided to have a little target practice. We didn't want to waste our arrows by embedding them in tree trunks, so we used a bale of hay as a target. Well, I must say that we hadn't lost any accuracy. The new arrows flew true. The only surprise came with their penetrating so deep into the bail that most of the shafts poked out the other side. The bow had powered them through five feet of compacted hay. Our bows and arrows were ready.

CHAPTER 9

CIRCLED CROSS RANCH

The skies looked to be flirting with snow as we headed out for the Circled Cross. Michael rode in a special rig behind Morning Star on Spirit Horse, while Moses sat astride the mare. He was bust-a-button proud in the buckskins she had made for him. I realized that it wouldn't be but another couple of years before I'd be teaching my son to shoot and guide him in learning how to hunt and camp.

Sure enough, as we approached the Freeman's ranch, flurries began falling. This was the third week of October, and the mountain tops were already wearing their snow blankets. While it wasn't looking to be a full-fledged storm, I was of a mind that we could see a couple of inches. Fortunately, the ground we covered was mostly flat prairie land, as footing for man and horse in the mountains could be treacherous during snow events. We were about a half mile from the ranch house, when Taabe joined us. His coat was already sparkling with flakes of snow.

George was standing out front as we reined in. "Y'all

picked a fine time to visit," he noted with a touch of sarcasm. He lit us up with his usual broad smile. "Who's the big man on the mare?" he asked with a nod toward Moses.

"Me ride," responded my son with a huge grin, as snowflakes fell upon him.

"Great to see y'all," I said. "Figured we'd bring some weather along with us."

* * *

Soon we had the horses stabled and were nestled in the warmth of the Freeman's home. Running Waters had prepared a wonderful feast with young Esmeralda's help. The cooking aromas were pleasantly overwhelming. Morning Star set Michael aside and pitched in, but most of the work had been done.

"*Ana o'a hi'it?*" said Running Waters, using the Comanche language as a sort of deference to me. She then turned to Morning Star. "*Wówaŋyaŋke,*" she invited in the Lakota tongue.

Had we known any Pawnee, we'd have responded in kind. We were all ready to eat.

We sat around the big oak table gracing the Freeman's kitchen. The table had seen a few years and had the gouges, scrapes, and scars to prove it. If it had a voice, that old table could tell plenty of fascinating stories. George blessed the meal, and everyone dug in as though they hadn't eaten in ages. George and I looked knowingly at each other as we anticipated our traditional post-meal gathering around the hearth. While faith was often discussed, on this occasion, there'd be more talk of the goings on with ranching and Indians across Wyoming Territory.

As we enjoyed the meal, I kept a watchful eye on Esmeralda. She was growing into a beautiful young lady. At fourteen, she was of age by frontier standards. She combined the best physical features of both George and Running Waters, as she bore his dark skin but her mother's Pawnee facial features. While her looks leaned toward her mother, her personality was more like her father. Would a White cowboy like Cutter suit her tastes? And would Cutter be attracted to her? I decided to not mention my matchmaking to anyone but create a situation in which they would meet. I had a long winter ahead to work that out.

After dinner, we gathered at the hearth. After George opened with a prayer, I broke the ice as it were. "What do you know of the Wyoming Stock Growers Association, George?"

Morning Star and Running Waters looked at me as though I had opened an unfit subject for this gathering.

"I want to know," said Esmeralda.

George smiled knowingly. "It's simple, Isa. Folks like you and me aren't welcome. Plus, the big ranchers resent smaller spreads like this one. Since you're raising horses and not taking their grazing lands or water, they'll leave you alone. If times get tough, like a big freeze or a long drought, they're going to give the smaller ranchers a hard time."

"What do you mean by hard time, Papa?" asked Esmeralda.

"They'd try to force us to sell out," replied George.

"You mean take it?" Esmeralda persisted.

"You upset daughter," said a concerned Running Waters.

George smiled gently. "It's the real world. God might throw some tough tests at us."

"Lakota, Cheyenne, and Arapaho were plenty test," contributed Morning Star.

I looked at George. "The men in Cheyenne have much money. They will use it to buy power and control. We must figure how to respond if what you suggest happens. Men like Teschemacher already apply strong influence over the three Cheyenne newspapers. While they play polo on their fancy eastern ponies, the newspapers tell folks how they should think." I took a long sip of coffee. "We must be prepared. Meanwhile, let's discuss the weeks ahead. The snow that followed us here is a sign of what is to come."

"We warm in cabins. Tatanka Iyotake's people freeze on reservation at Standing Rock Agency near Fort Yates," contributed Morning Star.

"Soldiers at Fort Laramie say they've moved them to Fort Randall. They fear he will stir trouble at Standing Rock," noted George.

"My people at Standing Rock," lamented Morning Star.

I briefly considered that we might journey to the reservation.

"What you think, Isa?" she pressed.

"A journey in winter would be foolish. The Lakota have endured many winters. They will survive this one." I caught her sad eyes. "We must consider our children. We should not risk a journey."

"Christmas will be here in a couple of months," ventured George in a vain attempt to change the subject.

Morning Star gave me a mournful look. "Isa right, but Awentia not happy." She hugged my arm.

The glory days of the Indian nations of the plains were ending. It was a harsh reality to overcome. Hunting grounds were disappearing, and populations were seriously reduced. The old traditions would soon be gone, especially as young men no longer knew the ways of the hunters and warriors.

My children and I were of a culture of human cross-breeding. Moses and Michael were half Lakota and half my mix of Comanche and White. Esmeralda was half Pawnee and half Black. Overriding this all was the fact that they were Americans. I had come to realize that we must overcome the cultural and racial differences that sought to divide and embrace a joining together under one banner, both of a nation and of faith.

"I want pony for Christmas," said Esmeralda out of the blue.

"Me ride horse," interjected Moses with a giggle.

"Maybe Esmeralda will get a horse for Christmas," said George with a grin. "But, it is better to give than to receive."

"Why, Papa," she asked.

"It gives folks pleasure to give gifts that make others happy," I noted.

"I like gifts," she insisted.

Running Waters rolled her eyes as though saying that she was yet too young to understand. "Wait until you have children, daughter," she counseled.

"I don't even have a man, Mama," lamented Esmeralda.

"If the snow isn't too bad come December, maybe we could have a big Christmas celebration at our spread." I offered. Aside from celebrating Christ's birth, I had in mind to put Cutter and Esmeralda together.

Morning Star gave me one of her *I know what you're thinking* looks.

We sat around for another hour talking about the

goings on in the region around Fort Laramie. George ultimately closed with some Bible verses.

* * *

Looking out across George's pastures next morning, we were greeted by a couple of inches of new fallen snow. It had stopped falling during the early morning hours and now graced us with a scene like a winter wonderland. The landscape was draped in powdery, almost delicate jewels of white. Gnarled and twisted tree limbs and thick shrubs were blunted, robed in winter's raiment. I stood in the doorway of George's house simply absorbing God's handiwork.

"What Isa see?" asked Morning Star, sidling up behind me.

"I see our destiny. I see Wyoming's destiny."

"Destiny?" she asked.

"Yes. It's God's decree for the world to come. We are part of it." I turned and kissed her.

"We better go home to meet this destiny," she teased.

We enjoyed a wonderful breakfast before setting out on the trail to our Laramie Cross Breed Ranch. It had been wonderful to visit with the Freeman family. He had been an important influence on my pa and, by extension, on me.

The sun on the new fallen snow made the landscape blinding. Snow blindness was a very real danger. George gifted us with goggles featuring horizontal slits across the eye holes. These significantly reduced the effect of extended exposure to the seemingly endless whiteness.

We took it easy, as we were in no hurry.

"You think Cutter like Esmeralda?" Morning Star

finally asked the question that had been lingering on her mind since last night.

I gave a *why not* shrug.

While it was dangerous to look directly into the sun, the brightness of the snow-covered landscape blazing back at us was nearly as blinding. The goggles were a godsend. The autumn had yet to deliver one of its surprise storms with winds that piled snow in drifts to a horse's withers. The present couple of inches made for slower going, owing to places that became slippery where snow turned to ice that covered rocks in the trail. While he protested a bit, I persuaded Moses to ride with me on my sure-footed steed, Mukue. He was as yet too inexperienced to be tackling the uncertain footing.

By the time we arrived at our home in mid-afternoon, most of the snow had melted. Yet, I had a premonition that we'd be seeing our first serious storm of the season sooner rather than later. We had nearly completed preparations for the coming winter. Plenty of feed had been stored for the livestock. While the horses would all be kept dry and relatively warm inside the stables and exercise arena, we'd extended the snow baffles that our friend George had invented to shelter our cattle.

* * *

The morning after our arrival home, Morning Star seemed sad.

"What troubles Awentia?" I asked. I suspected that it had to do with her Lakota family, but I wanted to hear it from her.

"My people at Standing Rock," she replied. "Winter come. Army no help."

Sadly, she was likely right. The US Army and the Indian agencies had done poorly by the terms of the treaties. Some of her Miniconjou Lakota people would starve if they didn't freeze to death for want of good blankets and shelter. The Lakota had, long before the arrival of the White man, spent many years surviving the frigid temperatures and heavy snows of the mountains. Game had always been plentiful, and the men were skilled hunters. This was not so true anymore. "Snow come soon," I responded. I was implying that the risks were too great to even think about helping them. The journey from here to the Standing Rock Agency through the snows of late autumn would entail more than three weeks each way. A load of food and blankets could nearly double the time.

She looked at me as though I'd let her down. "We help," she insisted.

In the first place, it would take several days to gather enough foodstuffs and blankets to help the Lakota. On the trail, we'd have to negotiate a half dozen ice-choked rivers and the rugged Badlands and Black Hills. By the time we'd near the encampment, we'd be pulling a heavy wagon through many feet of snow. "Such a journey would be very difficult for you and me on horseback. With children and a loaded wagon, it would be very risky." I chose not to say impossible.

Morning Star sighed and went to her beading loom.

My thoughts were full of sadness over her worries. The government had treated her people no better than mine. While my Comanche people didn't worry so much about snow, they too felt the pain of insufficient supplies. I felt her pain.

The Standing Rock Agency was supplied by Fort Yates situated on the Oahe Lake formed by damming the

Missouri River. The fort was north of where Morning Star's people were camped. Even if we were able to put together a rescue mission, we had no idea what we might encounter at the agency. We assumed that the Lakota were not receiving sufficient supplies, but we could be wrong. We'd take undue risk on a fool's errand. I walked over to her and placed my arm gently around her shoulders. "I will pray on this, Awentia," I assured her. I did reckon to put this matter in God's hands, though I doubted He'd test me in such a way.

CHAPTER 10

SNOWBOUND

Will Cutter was of a rangy build but a handsome lad. He took the leads of the team pulling the second wagon in our little Christmas caravan along the Oregon Trail to the Freeman spread. He was totally innocent about what I had in store for him. Joe Moon rode a big chestnut Quarter Horse alongside that wagon. Chester Donovan drove our lead wagon with Morning Star, our two sons, his wife Pearl, and their newborn daughter as passengers. I rode Mukue at point, making sure we encountered no obstacles.

Morning Star had mostly gotten over he concern with her people at the Standing Rock Agency. I had prayed on it and felt led to believe that we should not risk the journey at this time of the year. We would have to rely on the resourcefulness yet remaining with the Lakota. To ease her discomfort, I rode to Fort Laramie and persuaded Captain Hayes to get a message to Fort Yates encouraging them in their supply duties to the Lakota encampment. Of course, I couldn't know that Fort Yates was hurting for its own supplies.

We'd left early on the day before Christmas and arrived at the Circled Cross Ranch late that afternoon. I kept an eye on our backtrail during the journey, not the ground we rode on but the skies. There was a dark foreboding cloud cover building over the Laramie Mountains, and I didn't like the look of it one little bit.

"Welcome," called out George, as we reined in at his home. "Merry Christmas!" he declared.

Donovan saw to the unloading of the wagons and stabling of the horses, while the women and children climbed from the lead wagon and headed inside to enjoy the radiant warmth of the Freeman hearth and the aromas wafting from Running Waters' stove. Esmeralda was helping and looked divine in a form-fitting white buckskin dress decorated with intricate beadwork designs.

George joined me as I saw to Mukue in the barn.

"I can smell Running Waters' fine cooking from here, George," I joked.

"Wait until you taste it," he rejoined. He then hunkered down close in. "I get a sense that you're up to something, Isa."

I looked around to be sure no one was within earshot. "I'm fixing to find out if my young ranch hand Will Cutter might have a fancy for Esmeralda," I whispered. There, my secret was out.

George's eyebrows went up. "She's not taken a fancy to anyone so far as I know," he said with a devious smile and some rubbing together of his hands. "Guess we'll see what happens."

"Cutter's awkward around womenfolk."

Stifling a grin, George added knowingly, "If there's any feelings, she'll bring them out."

* * *

Running Waters had decorated the interior of their home beautifully with pine boughs, red bows, and pinecones. Somehow, probably from a passing wagon train, she'd managed to get her hands on some silvery stuff she called tinsel. It was sparkly and gave a festive air to their home.

The Freemans had laid out what I figured to be enough food to feed the troops at Fort Laramie. They sure knew how to put on a Christmas feed. All told and counting kids and ranch hands, there were sixteen of us nestled around the table.

George was now in on my plan. He encouraged the ranch hands to not sit bunched together by telling Cutter to sit opposite Esmeralda and placing him between me and Donovan's wife, Pearl. He was pretty much forced to look directly across the table. George and I waited with heightened anticipation as to what might happen when and if their eyes met.

After George blessed the meal, we began to dig in.

I happened to glance to my right to ask Pearl something when I caught a slack-jawed, wide-eyed Cutter staring straight ahead at Esmeralda. His fork was poised between his plate and mouth. For her part, she had averted her eyes.

"Grub, okay?" I asked him. I might as well have been talking to a stone wall.

Now, Esmeralda was no ordinary fourteen-year-old. Aside from being book-learned, she was strikingly beautiful in an exotic sort of way. Her dark eyes flitted around in just about any direction except at Cutter.

I looked over at George.

He, too, had been keeping an eye on the two while he talked with his lead ranch hand Hap Evans.

I winked at Morning Star, and she smiled back knowingly.

There were some feelings welling up between the two, and it was tickling our fancies to no end. We'd done what we could, so now had to take care to let God's will take hold.

Suddenly, Esmeralda looked across the table directly at Cutter. "Will Cutter, is Jesus Christ your Savior?"

I nearly dropped my knife and fork. A silence swept the table as everyone awaited Cutter's reply.

For a second, Cutter seemed befuddled. The question obviously rocked him, given both its content and the shock of it being the very first thing she said to him. She'd barely acknowledged his existence before this moment at Christmas dinner. He gathered himself together and shot an appraising look back at her. "Yep. How about you, Esmeralda Freeman?"

I don't think she expected him to boldly return the question, but she never flinched. Instead, she delivered a smile that said she wanted to learn more about Will Cutter.

"How come y'all aren't eating?" boomed George.

Amid laughs and guffaws, everyone returned to enjoying the feast. I wasn't the only one in on the matchmaking.

* * *

Soon, the little ones were sacked out in various niches around the house while we adults gathered around at the hearth.

Perhaps it was the Comanche in me, but I sensed

that it had grown dark a bit early. Everyone else was caught up in singing and the general revelry. I snuck over to a front window and gazed out to the west. There was supposed to be a full moon, though I could barely make it out. About this time, a pine tree came blowing across the expanse between the house and the barn.

I banged the hilt of my Bowie knife on the table to get everyone's attention.

Questioning eyes stared back at me.

"Folks, there's a blizzard coming in!" I announced.

Everyone rushed to the front windows. A heavy snow was already being driven horizontally by stiff winds. If it was typical of the winter blizzards around these parts, we were seeing only the milder beginnings of the storm.

George stepped back with a big smile. "Well, folks, it appears that we're about to be snowbound for a while. Let's get back to singing." He promptly led the way back to the hearth.

Unnoticed were Cutter and Esmeralda off to the side and carrying on some sort of conversation. Cutter was talking up a storm, and she was listening intently with eyes that said she'd found herself a man.

I thought back to the tests Morning Star and I had endured throughout our courtship. Cutter and Esmeralda likely wouldn't have to worry about fighting off Cheyenne savages and traveling rugged mountainous terrain. Now, we led a different life. My warrior woman wife had become a mother and guardian of our domestic bliss. She was still tough but settled down. That having been said, I appreciated having her strength in standing beside me to fight off any threats.

George had surely taught Esmeralda how to ride and shoot, just as Running Waters had guided her with cooking, sewing, and the myriad tasks of running a household.

Upon consideration, I figured that I needed to *sweeten the pot*, so to speak. Cutter needed to offer Esmeralda something more than his job as a ranch hand. I knew of a six-hundred-and-forty-acre parcel between our spread and Guernsey's. I was of a mind to help him acquire that and gift him with a couple of head of cattle to get a ranch started. I talked it over with Morning Star and Donovan, and they thought it would be a great idea. I felt that families taking root was important toward taming the frontier. With the railroads expanding and towns springing up, it seemed to make sense. There was a destiny about it; a Wyoming destiny.

* * *

It wasn't taking long for the snow to begin piling up against fences and buildings. I thought briefly on the wagon trains that had stopped for the winter at The Emigrant's Washtub. They had to be relieved to have not attempted to continue on through the mountain passes. They'd no doubt heard of the Donner wagon train stuck in the snow drifts of the Sierra Madre nearly forty years back. Half of the eighty-seven men, women, and children had perished. Some say that they resorted to cannibalism to survive. The very thought caused me an involuntary shudder, though I was all too aware that my ancestors and other tribes had practiced various degrees of cannibalism.

George had laid out the colored ropes from the house to the barn and the bunkhouse. Since the house was crowded, we sent all the ranch hands except Donovan out to the bunkhouse. George, Donovan, and I went out and made certain everything in the barn was secure. We could hear cattle bawling as they huddled near the protective snow baffles. So long as the beeves had something to say, all was well. I must say that I was right glad to have my bearskin coat.

The toughest part of sending the ranch hands to the bunkhouse was separating Cutter and Esmeralda. Of course, it made sense to keep their budding acquaintanceship from getting too warm too soon. From Cutter's point of view, the warmth of the bunkhouse likely seemed cold compared to his feelings for the exotic-looking woman he'd just met.

* * *

We remained pinned down at the Circled Cross Ranch for the next three days, as the blizzard raged through. It ended at just about the time we figured it might never pass on.

At sunrise on the morning after the blizzard, Morning Star and I took a gander outside to decide whether we should head home. Even on the Oregon Trail, we could see from a distance that the snow was deep and the going would be tough. I figured the snow would be at the level of the beds of our wagons. It might be days before the snow melted sufficiently to permit passage, and that was assuming temperatures at or above freezing.

"Snow deep," observed Morning Star as she stood wrapped in a blanket and nestled under my arm while she sipped hot coffee.

I nodded in agreement. "We might be here for a while longer."

As though on cue, George strode over. "Not to worry.

We have plenty enough food and firewood," he assured us.

I motioned over to where Esmeralda was talking animatedly with her mother. "Somebody seems especially perky today."

George laughed. "I can't understand why."

"Dare we invite the men in for a meal?" I ventured.

Morning Star shook her head. "Teach patience."

"There's something to be said for that," added George. "The feelings of new love can blaze too hot too soon, then cool just as quick. It's like wine, as the better wine ages a bit."

"Maybe it's time that I go have a chat with young Mr. Cutter," I offered.

Morning Star smiled and kissed my arm lightly. "Isa wise."

"I'll join you, if you don't mind," added George.

I shook my head. "I think it better to not overwhelm the lad. I'll do it myself, George."

He agreed, and I grabbed my bearskin coat. I negotiated the two-foot-deep snow to the bunkhouse. Once there, I greeted the ranch hands and asked Cutter to come help me in the barn to get him away from prying ears.

"What's up, boss?" he asked, rubbing his chilled hands together and shivering a bit in the cold.

"Aside from you needing a warmer coat, I just reckoned to share a bit of advice if you're up for it."

"You're going to talk with me about Esmeralda, ain't you?" he responded.

"Nope," I replied.

Still shivering, he gave me a curious look.

"Obviously, you two are getting it on, but that's not what I wanted to talk about." I handed him a shovel and grabbed one myself. I began to nonchalantly muck a stall.

"What then?" Cutter pressed.

"There's a parcel between the Laramie Cross Breed Ranch and Charles Guernsey's ranch. I wondered whether it might interest you to have your own spread." I kept mucking.

Cutter paused. "I ain't got enough money for that, boss."

"What if I helped?" I paused and leaned against my shovel.

"You'd do that?" he asked.

"I reckon it might give you a bit more to offer a woman than being a forty-dollar-a-month ranch hand. I might even toss in a couple of beeves." I watched Cutter's jaw drop.

"Watch out," I chuckled. "Your tongue might freeze."

"You'd do that for me?" He was downright amazed.

"Let's see what happens with you and the young woman over yonder, Will. The offer stands, if things… well…if things develop."

"I'd be eternally grateful, boss," he finally responded.

"I don't know about eternal, but the near future will do for now," I added with a laugh. "I'll send a couple of the men over to help here while I head back to the house." I left Cutter standing there with a look of gratefulness frozen across his face. He returned to mucking.

* * *

My smile upon reentering the house told everyone but a clueless Esmeralda that my little get-together with Cutter had gone as planned. Now, it was up to the vagaries of courtship and God's will, though I sensed things would be moving along right quickly.

Morning Star sidled up to me. "Maybe two, maybe three days?" Despite the Freeman's hospitality, she was as anxious to get home as I was. We had our livestock to check on, though I felt confident that they'd be fine.

"Long as it doesn't snow again," I replied. "It's going to be a tough haul." Despite the Freeman's hospitality, the tight quarters tended to fray nerves a bit. The sooner we could head for home, the better.

CHAPTER 11

TROUBLE LEAST EXPECTED

Being snowbound at the Freeman's spread had been quite an experience. A true test of our civility and faith comes with being thrust together at close quarters for an extended period. The trek home, through foot-deep snow, had been uneventful though slow going. By the time we reached home, Cutter was already pining for Esmeralda.

April finally rolled around. I'd read *Ben Hur* three times and *Locke's Treatices* two times. I also read the book Morning Star had borrowed, George Belden's *Twelve Years Among the Wild Indians of the Plains*. That led to interesting chats, as we found ourselves occasionally disagreeing with the White general's effort to experience and describe our tribal culture. These books did make me determined to build our own library. We were teaching Moses to read, and Michael soon would be old enough, and we wanted plenty of book learning for both of them.

I was about to saddle Mukue for a ride to our south pasture when George Freeman came galloping in with his ranch hands Hap and Dred. As he reined in, I noted that his usual smile of greeting wasn't to be seen. "Where is she, Isa?"

I shot back a questioning gaze. "Who?"

"Esmeralda," he replied. "She's run off with that fool ranch hand of yours."

"Whoa, George! How can you be sure? I saw Cutter not a half hour ago heading north with Donovan," I replied as level-headed as I could muster.

"Well, she headed this way," he insisted.

I scratched my chin thoughtfully. "Cool down, George. This isn't like you. You've taught her better than to run off, so there must be something else afoot."

"Such as?" he challenged.

"I've got a hunch. Let's take a ride north toward where Cutter and Donovan were heading."

George reluctantly agreed.

About this time, Taabe appeared, and that gave me an idea. "Let's make this easier," I suggested. I strode into the bunkhouse and grabbed one of Cutter's shirts. Upon emerging, I gave Taabe a good sniff. We were now an official search party.

I climbed into Mukue's saddle, and off we went with Taabe loping along well out in front of us. My intuition told me that what we'd encounter would be far more innocent than George feared. I could be wrong, but I preferred to think positive.

George was as unhappy as I'd ever seen him, and Hap and Dred were uncharacteristically close-mouthed. If their boss was concerned, they were obliged to follow suit.

It's about three miles from my home to the North Platte River. Taabe stopped atop a knoll about a quarter mile from the Oregon Trail. As I approached with

George and the others, he gave a couple of yips. Off in the distance, I could make out the hazy green of freshly budding cottonwoods along the riverbank. I drew my telescope and slowly swept the trees.

George, Hap, and Dred reined in behind me. "What are you stopping for?" asked George.

I motioned George forward and passed him the telescope. "See the taller of those cottonwoods. Focus in on that spot."

He reluctantly lifted the telescope and focused on the spot I'd pointed out.

Well, there sat Chester Donovan, his horse grazing close by while he kept an eye on a pair of picnickers.

George collapsed the telescope and sheepishly handed it back to me. "She should have told me," he finally blurted.

Esmeralda was a grown woman by frontier standards and surely had a mind of her own. Plus, the strong emotions surrounding love tended to override anything resembling common sense. She's made up her mind, and that was that.

"You haven't asked my advice, but I'd be saving any scolding for when she got home," I urged. "Donovan's keeping an eye on them, so you needn't fear any trouble."

George gave me a long look before finally cracking a slight smile. "Thanks, Isa. I should have trusted her. In fact, it appears that your man Will Cutter is an honorable sort."

With that, we parted ways. I called Taabe in, and we watched George and his ranch hands head for home. I took a long, wishful look at the two lovebirds and made a mental note to take Morning Star on a picnic soon.

I turned Mukue for home. My senses told me there'd be a wedding soon.

* * *

I rode right on past the house toward the south pastures. I figured to tell Morning Star later about George's concerns and the outcome. I reckoned that I could likely embellish it a tad, perhaps adding a touch of humor.

Taabe loped alongside as I urged Mukue to a canter. I took in the fresh mountain air of early spring. Off in the distance, the peaks of the Laramie Range were still snow-capped. They'd be that way for a few weeks yet. Meanwhile, they offered a contrast to the budding greenery at lower altitudes. The lodgepole pines were green year-round, but the aspens, cottonwoods, willows, and boxelders were just busting from the winter drab. It was as though new life had spring up almost overnight. God sure outdid himself up here.

The winter had treated us to plenty of snow, but we'd endured. So far as we'd been able to tell, only two beeves had been lost, and the horses were all fine. Foaling would be underway soon. The cattle had been lost to wolves. It reminded me of Taabe's roots. While he was a loyal companion, he was nevertheless an apex hunter. While he never hunted our cattle, I knew that other wolves lurked in the woodlands and prairies surrounding us. With the challenges of finding food during the winter, a vulnerable cow could be mighty tasty and easy hunting. Fortunately, there were plenty of buffalo, elk, and other prey, and they weren't generally close to humans. I suppose we should be thankful that the wolves of the wild had an aversion to the likes of me, except Taabe, of course.

We were about three miles from home under a cloudless sky and breathing crystal clear air when I spotted five riders heading toward me about a mile out. I saw no packhorses, so they were traveling light. Why and from where? And why were they riding across my ranch?

I pulled up atop a rise in the prairie. It was a cool day with a westerly breeze adding a slight chill, so I was glad that Morning Star had insisted that I wear a heavier set of buckskins.

The riders were between a quarter and a half mile away when the lead rider spotted me. Now, this was still very much the frontier, and these sorts of encounters required the exercise of caution. There was no telling whether friend or foe stood before you. The five came to a halt and began eyeing me curiously. While they outnumbered me, they had surely seen my tan buckskins and the long dark braids hanging over my ears and were trying to figure out whether I might be riding point for a band of hostile Indians.

I raised my right hand with palm facing them.

They didn't move but talked among themselves. A couple of them were quite animated and pointed my way. Given the way their faces contorted, they appeared concerned, even fearful.

I pulled my telescope from my saddlebags for a closer look. What I saw seemed innocent enough, though there was no obvious clue as to what they were up to.

The sun must have caught the brass casing of my telescope, because they suddenly all looked my way, talk ceased, and rifles were drawn. Blessedly, they didn't move, but the rifles were pointed in my general direction.

I put the telescope away and raised my hand once again. I admit that my heart was pounding a tad faster. What were they up to?

* * *

My pa had a policy of ranch hands heading out in pairs. About now, I was wishing that I'd exercised the same policy. An abundance of caution told me to head home, while curiosity kept me unmoving.

Finally, the lead rider and one other headed in my direction with rifle butts on their hips and muzzles pointed skyward. They did not yet appear threatening, but neither did they seem to be looking to make nice. They rode to within about fifty feet of me.

"You an Injun?" asked the lead rider.

"I'm Isa O'Toole, and I own the property y'all are riding across."

"A breed, are you?" he asked.

I kept a straight face and ignored the question. "Who are you and where do you go?"

"Any White folk around that we can talk with?" His question cast further light on the man's prejudice.

I was realizing that this situation could easily turn into trouble. "Who are you, and what's your business?" I insisted.

The two lowered their rifles into a position to easily shoot at me. "None of your business. How many scalps you got, Injun?"

This was turning nasty. If I moved for my rifle, they'd surely gun me down.

Taabe appeared. He gave a long look at the two riders and emitted a low guttural growl.

"That's a wolf, ain't it?" queried the lead rider with a hint of fear.

"He only attacks humans that bother me," I stated flatly.

The second man brought his rifle up and aimed it at Taabe. He couldn't miss from where he sat his horse, and I was powerless to defend my wolf companion.

"Don't!" I exclaimed just as the man flew from his saddle. Then, I heard the report. It was a booming sound like from a buffalo gun.

The lead rider's horse reared, dumping him to the ground. Taabe was on him in a flash.

"Taabe! Taabe!" I hollered. I grabbed my Spencer rifle, dismounted, and managed to free the man from the vice-like grip Taabe had on his arm.

"Get him away! Get him away!" the man pleaded. His bloodied arm was obviously broken, and he'd hit the ground hard after being dumped from his mount.

Now, the other three riders headed toward us. They hadn't gone but a few yards when a second shot boomed across the prairie and a horse fell from beneath one of the riders. The other two pulled up and looked to be at a loss for what to do.

The man whom Taabe had attacked groveled at my feet. "H-h-help me," he pleaded.

Taabe stood at my side, teeth bared at the man.

"Wagh!" came a cry from my left.

I knew that voice. Sure enough, Wally Wallace came walking toward me with his horse and mule in tow. Our old mountain man friend had appeared just in time. He calmly reloaded his newly acquired Sharps rifle as he headed my way with a big grin on his face. "Danged good shootin'!" he exclaimed.

"About time you showed up," I said nonchalantly.

A low moan came from the man still lying at my feet. He was in rough shape. "Don't be scalping me," he begged.

I drew my Bowie knife and gave him a look that said I was ready to lift his hair. I re-sheathed my knife. "Tell your friends to drop their guns and ride in here real careful-like," I directed him.

"I don't take no orders from Injuns," he managed to insist through obvious pain.

Wally let loose a booming shot over the heads of the man's remaining companions. "Drop them guns an' git yer hides in here!" he commanded.

I looked down at the wounded and decidedly prejudiced man. I felt a combination of pity and disgust.

"One of your partners is dead, you're short a horse, and you're in no position to bargain," I told him straight out. "Now, who are you and what's your business?"

By now, the other three had joined our little gathering. Wally had reloaded the Sharps, and I had my rifle handy. There'd be no further gunplay if I could help it. I looked out at the three men standing in front of their two horses. "You," I said with a motion to one of them, "go drag your friend's body over here and fetch his horse." I turned to the man who'd had his cayuse shot from under him. "Your friend here seems to have trouble with his voice. I haven't heard who y'all are and what your business is."

There was fear in his eyes, but he didn't look inclined to talk.

I glanced over at Wally and winked. "Well, I guess I'll just have to get on with the scalping." With that, I unsheathed my Bowie knife and stepped closer to their wounded leader.

"W-w-wait!" said the wounded man. "I be John Granger. D-d-don't be scalping me." Tears filled his terror-stricken eyes. "We lost our packhorses to a bear. We be headed to The Emigrant's Washtub to catch a train to Oregon."

I looked over at Wally and shrugged.

He laughed and gave the wounded man a hard eye. "Yuh had better hope thet the dumbest man on God's earth don't die, cause that'd put yuh in his shoes. This man yer callin' an Injun is one of the toughest men I ever did meet. He be so tough, he'd take on a nest of rattlers an' spot 'em the first bite. Yer lucky tuh be livin'.'"

Granger wasn't acting so tough anymore. His eyes focused fearfully on the Bowie knife still in my hand.

I fully appreciated Wally's humor, and it seemed to have a positive effect on the four men whom we now looked to be holding as prisoners. "What do we do with this bunch?" I asked Wally.

"Don't rightly know," he replied. "We could string 'em up, but thet might be overkill an' waste good rope." He gave a guffaw at his humor.

"P-p-please. We're sorry, Mr. O'Toole, sir. Let us bury our friend and go our way." The wounded man was finding some contrition.

By now, the dead man had been draped across the saddle of one of the horses. That left four men and three available horses. It was roughly a fifteen-mile walk to The Emigrant's Washtub. While I was, by my faith, a forgiving man, I had my limits, and they were testing my patience. Had it not been for Wally's appearance, I might be pushing up daisies. I glanced at Wally, and he shrugged as though it was fully my call. "Mr. Granger, this is your lucky day. Seems that we have no lawman around here just yet. We could escort y'all to Fort Laramie, but the Army wouldn't know what to do with you. You sure as shooting won't be tainting the soil of my ranch with your friend's body. That tree line over yonder to the west runs up toward The Emigrant's Washtub. I'm not sure what folks up there would want with you. Maybe you can hitch on with a train headed west."

"Y-y-you letting us go free?" asked an amazed John Granger.

"Not quite. You're leaving your hardware here with me, and I'll oblige y'all to take off your boots. But for the horse carrying your dead friend, I'll be taking your horses up to The Emigrant's Washtub so they'll be plenty rested when y'all get there." I had to work hard to suppress a satisfied grin at what would become their great discomfort.

"Yuh makin' us walk?" queried one of the men.

"Well, it's your choice," I replied.

"Choice?" asked Granger.

"Either walk or be introduced to those trees over yonder. I do have plenty enough rope."

The men gulped pretty much in unison. They were hardly in a position to negotiate, and they weren't quite certain as to whether I was serious about hanging them.

"Y'all likely have kinfolk somewhere, and I'd rightly dislike the hassle of trying to reach out to them about your untimely passing." How I managed to deliver this with a straight face took all I could muster, especially with Wally obviously holding back a belly laugh.

The men slipped off their boots.

"Y'all get started. We'll gather your guns, boots, and horses. It's only about fifteen miles, and they'll be waiting for you." I motioned for them to go. "Wait a minute," I called out. Granger was hurting pretty bad, and I felt a little pity for him. I took one of the rifles, unloaded it, and broke it in two over a nearby rock. "Get over here, Granger, and sit."

He obeyed.

With the rifle barrel and a couple of strips of cloth torn from Granger's own shirt, I fashioned a splint for his arm. He howled some with pain but endured my efforts. He bled a bit more, but his arm was secured.

"Why are you doing this?" he winced.

"Just be thankful that y'all attacked a God-fearing man." I smiled at him. "Guess you could say the White man in me tended to your arm while the Comanche would've scalped you. Now, join your friends. It's a long walk, and the daylight is still short."

Wally and I watched the men limp and stagger away in their bare feet. We then went about collecting the rifles, revolvers, and boots. "You of a mind to come visit us?" I asked.

"I be sort of passin' through but wouldn't be mindin' some fine grub," he replied.

"Well, if you're of a mind to join me, we can make the Washtub right quickly and be home just after sunset. Shucks, it's a fine day for a ride."

We mounted up and headed north. It took a mere twenty minutes until we passed the men stepping real careful-like on their trip to The Emigrant's Washtub. We waved as we rode on by. They didn't wave back. I suspected that they didn't have kind things to say about us as we rode from sight.

"What brought you back to this neck of the woods, Wally?"

"When yer up in them thar mountains, yuh jus' go with my mule's druthers. He done led me back thisaway," he deadpanned. Then, he smiled. "Had a hankerin' fer yer woman's cookin'."

That sure made better sense, though he was a wandering man. "So, the good Lord's seen fit to let you keep your hair," I teased.

"Ain't hardly no savages tuh come after it," he lamented with brutal honesty.

I couldn't help but notice how the years in the wild were taking their toll on my friend. The creases in his face were deeper, and his hair whiter. Wounds and falls led him to ride more than walk. His way of life had ended decades back, yet he relentlessly pursued the life of a mountain man. Trapping produced ever fewer beaver pews, and game in general was ever less plentiful. Yet, Wally Wallace was a man of the mountains of the frontier, a fitting testament to its enduring majesty; a legacy, if you will. "The Comanche in me would be pleased to chase you, if you like," I said with a chuckle.

"An' yuh'd likely ketch me," he laughed. He glanced at my necklace. "Looks like bears ain't safe with you aroun'."

"He put up a great fight." I reckoned that was explanation enough.

He gave me *the eye*.

"Nearly killed me," I admitted.

Wally nodded. "How's the horse bizness?"

"God's been treating us right. Blessed me with Mukue here, and we have three ranch hands and a bunch of two-year-old Quarter Horses about ready to sell."

"An' Awentia?" he asked.

"Pretty as ever. I married up, Wally." I anticipated his next question. "Moses has learned to ride, and Michael is growing like weeds in a corn patch. We've begun book learning them."

* * *

We reached The Emigrant's Washtub to find a wagon train pulling in. Wally and I waited for them to circle up before seeking out the wagon master.

We rode up slowly to the wagon circle with the four

horses in tow. An elderly woman was unhitching a team of oxen. They were strong, reliable animals, but made for slow going on the trail. "Pardon, ma'am, is your wagon master about?"

"Who you be?" she asked.

"Well, the owners of these nags will be along in a few hours, and we reckoned to tell the wagon master about them," I explained.

"He got snake bit and died," she lamented.

"Who's leading this outfit?" I queried.

"We been followin' the wagon ruts for the past week." She motioned to a tall man herding horses into a remuda. "Slim over yonder's been pretty much head man, but he's a greenhorn."

"Well, get him over here, if you'd be so kind."

The woman ambled over to close to Slim, yelled to him, and he headed our direction.

"What can I do for you?" he asked in an accent I couldn't place.

"The lady here says y'all lost your wagon master, and you've taken on the job. You up to that?" I asked.

"Why are you asking, and what are you about?" he responded.

I'd nearly forgotten why we'd come. "My name is Isa O'Toole. I own a ranch over yonder. My friend here is Wally Wallace. We were bringing these horses because the owners are headed this way, and they might be a bit of trouble."

"Trouble?" he asked. "How's they come to be on foot?"

"Well, they had some hard feelings about my heritage, and I had to defend myself. My friend here saved my skin." I let this sink in. "I'm afraid one of them won't be seeing any tomorrows. They said they were fixing to go to Oregon."

Slim glanced over at the horses and noticed the boots hanging from the saddle horns. "They barefoot?"

"Pretty much. We figured walking barefoot would take the fight out of them."

"You say they're violent men?" asked Slim.

"I expect they behave better around White folks," I replied. "Y'all will have to judge for yourselves. We told them we'd leave their horses, boots, and guns here." I scanned the wagon circle. "You look to have enough strong men here. The way ahead will be tough going."

"How tough?" asked the woman. "I be a widow, an' tryin' to begin anew."

"At least twice as tough as from where y'all have been. But plenty of folks have made it to Oregon. Just stay on the trail."

Slim gave me an appraising gaze. I suppose he was judging my buckskins and general frontiersman aura. "You sound as though you know the trail. Could you lead us through?"

I looked over at Wally, who put on a big grin as though knowing my answer. "Nope. Afraid not. I've got a ranch here and a wife and children to tend to." At that, an idea came to me. "Now, Wally here," I said with a chuckle, expecting Wally's answer.

"I could git yuh through them tough passes," offered Wally.

I was fully surprised. I'd missed that Wally and the woman had been flirting with each other while I talked with Slim. Now, I could see the twinkle in their eyes. "You up to missing Awentia's cooking?" I teased.

"There be a late snow headin' in," said Wally, pointing to clouds rolling in above the Laramie Mountains. "Train be settin' here fer a day or two. I got time fer some good grub. Maybe the missus here might cook some up." He was nothing if not forward, as the woman blushed at his offer.

Slim seemed relieved. "You'll do it?" he said, seeking to confirm Wally's offer.

Wally laid a sheepish smile on me and raised his hands palms up as though helpless to resist. "See yuh agin right soon, Isa." He walked off arm in arm with the widow lady.

I turned back to Slim. "I think y'all will be in good hands."

Slim took the reins of the horses we'd led in and waved as I rode off.

I wondered how those four wayward souls were doing, as they traipsed barefoot across the prairie. Hopefully, they'd arrive at The Emigrant's Washtub before the snow. I felt a tad sorry for them, but while forgiveness was in my heart, wrongdoing demanded punishment. Another man might have strung them up.

CHAPTER 12

HUNTER VS. PREY

As Morning Star placed dinner on the table before me, and the boys listened with rapt attention, I described the day's events. While concern spread across their faces during my description of the threatening encounter with the wayward travelers, they wound up laughing at Wally's fate. The boys had yet to experience Wally, and I hoped that one day he'd stroll across our threshold and share tales of his adventures.

We did have a wedding to prepare for. Cutter and Esmeralda had made the commitment, and the ladies were all atwitter with preparations for the event.

The Laramie Cross Breed Ranch was abuzz with mares foaling, two-year-olds being saddle-broke, and stallions mating. We had received several inquiries about our Quarter Horses from outfits in Cheyenne. Apparently, Charles Goodnight had been getting the word out. While I was still of a mind to build our cattle holdings in Texas, there seemed to be a sense of destiny here in Wyoming.

* * *

Well, the wedding day popped up right sooner than any of us menfolk expected. It's funny how women seem to have a better sense of these things. Cutter was probably the only male paying attention.

The Freeman's had laid out a big spread at their place. Hap constructed an archway under which the couple would be wed. Ribbons and bows were strung about, and flower centerpieces decorated the serving tables. So long as the weather held, it would be a lovely day. I found myself especially taken with a touch that Morning Star had come up with. Off in a grove of cottonwoods to the north of George's house, she'd recruited our ranch hands to build a teepee for the wedded couple's first night. It was beautifully done and brought back memories of our wedding night in the Lakota encampment.

I actually shucked my usual buckskins and dressed up in a suit. I rejected the tie, replacing it with a red bandana. I even polished my boots for the occasion. Morning Star donned a beautiful blue cotton dress with colorfully beaded white moccasins. Her long hair braids were twisted gracefully atop her head. She looked…well, it would be all I could do to keep my hands off her.

Running Waters made a stunningly dazzling white wedding dress for Esmeralda. In a word, she was *gorgeous*. She was pretty anyway, so the dress was sort of like gilding a lily.

George even got an Army photographer from Fort Laramie to come take pictures of the event for posterity.

Guests began arriving, and the grounds were soon packed with horses and wagons. Captain Hayes brought an honor guard of troopers from the fort to lend an air of military spit and polish to the occasion. George yearned to give away the bride, so had recruited the Fort Laramie chaplain to officiate. I didn't take a formal count, but I estimated about fifty guests plus children.

Once everyone was seated, Hap with his harmonica and Dred with his banjo opened up with some sort of march. George escorted Esmeralda down the aisle while all the ladies beamed with joy and the men smiled, mostly with thoughts of how lucky Cutter was.

"Ladies and gentlemen. We are gathered," began the chaplain.

A shot rang out, and a bullet grazed the archway just over the chaplain's head. Everybody ducked for cover. Cutter, Esmeralda, and the chaplain stood frozen in time for a second shot to nick the shoulder of Cutter's coat. They dove to the ground with Cutter protectively on top of Esmeralda. Blessedly, whoever was shooting was at too great a distance to get off an accurate shot.

I was first to scan the area and caught the haze of blue gun smoke hanging in the air near some willows on the south bank of the North Platte River. It was a good distance off. We were lucky thus far that the shooter hadn't hit anyone.

Captain Hayes, George, and my ranch hands, other than Cutter, headed for our horses and wagons to grab whatever weapons we could lay our hands upon. I'd brought Mukue tethered behind our wagon, so quickly saddled up. In but minutes, we had what amounted to a posse ready to pursue whoever was taking shots at us. Another bullet whistled past us as we lit out for the shooter. It didn't take long to arrive at the spot where the shooter had knelt. He had vanished. From what sign I could find, he'd headed across the river and was hightailing it northward.

"He's gone," I stated matter-of-factly.

"I'll muster a patrol and chase him down," said Hayes confidently.

I looked over at George and the rest of the posse. "Whoever this is will be long gone by the time a patrol is put together. I know the country he's headed into, and there are plenty of places to set an ambush."

George was seething a bit over the interruption of his daughter's day, but understood my caution. "What do you propose, Isa?"

"The coward who shot at us won't be back today. Let's go back, settle folks down, and get Will and Esmeralda hitched." I looked off in the direction to which the shooter had escaped. "I'll track him down later. He's in a hurry and will leave plenty of sign."

Reluctantly, our well-intended posse headed back to continue the ceremony.

* * *

With the interruption passed, a shaken Cutter and Esmeralda took their wedding vows, and the celebration began. Most guests soon forgot the brush with violence and lost themselves in the revelry surrounding wishing the newlyweds a wonderful future together, though George and I took turns keeping watch.

I took Morning Star aside. "Awentia, I must hunt whoever shot at us."

She shook her head, as she knew me well. "Blue coats no find," she lamented the hard truth.

"I will be careful." You'd better believe I figured to be careful. I had no idea whom I was up against. Given the shooter's poor marksmanship, I found myself cautiously optimistic.

"Are you going after that man?" interrupted Captain Hayes. "I can send a patrol with you."

For all his time out here on the frontier, the captain hadn't learned the basic rudiments of hunting. If I wanted to chase a wild animal, there'd be nothing like the rattle and jangle of sabers to get the beast on the run. "Thanks just the same, Captain. This is a one-man task."

He seemed to understand, bowing courteously to Morning Star and heading back to the celebration.

"We go home tonight. Pack for hunt," said Morning Star.

"I'll head out first thing in the morning." I said it confidently, though I hoped I wasn't underestimating my prey. Since I knew the place along the river that he'd fired from, I'd have a decent starting point to pick up sign.

After seeing Esmeralda and Cutter off to their teepee for their first night together, we headed for home. We'd have spent the night but for my commitment to hunting that shooter. The wagons made for slow going, and we arrived in the early morning hours under the dim light of moon and stars. I hoped to catch a couple of hours of shuteye before heading out.

While I slept, Morning Star put the children to bed and went about pulling together all I would need for the trail. Doggone, but she was an awesome wife.

The shooter will have had nearly a full day's head start. There'd been no rain, so I figured that my experience-honed tracking abilities would be put to good use. I didn't yet know whether my prey knew the countryside.

* * *

I'd slept solidly, so awakened rested and ready for the hunt. I had acquired a .45 caliber Marlin Model 1881 that had become popular. However, I wasn't taking any chances, so I also brought my trusty bow with a quiver and about two dozen arrows. My Colt Peacemaker was holstered at my hip. I was a walking armory. Morning Star had packed enough jerky that I wouldn't be starving. She threw in some fresh-baked bear sign that I'd likely finish before I reached the shooter's perch.

"Isa be safe," cautioned Morning Star as we shared a lover's kiss.

I nodded. "Chester and the boys should handle the ranch," I assured her. I knew that she'd actually be in charge.

Taabe arrived, letting me know that I wouldn't be doing any tracking without him. How could I complain?

I mounted Mukue and headed for the Oregon Trail from which I'd turn eastward. The sun eased its way up on the horizon ahead of me in all its golden glory. There wasn't a cloud in the sky. It would be a perfect day for a hunt. I figured that the shooter would likely keep to the lowlands, since snow still capped the mountain tops. The streams would be running heavy from snow melt, so it remained to be seen whether my prey would try to hide his trail by wading through the rushing waters.

As we rode along at an easy walk, I thought back on how Wally might have made out with that elderly widow. That in turn led me to wonder how the wagon train had handled the four travelers who had caused me so much trouble. By now, they were likely well into the roughest parts of the Oregon Trail, negotiating passes in higher elevations that still held some snow. I reckoned we'd begun seeing the last of wagon trains, as the railroads could take folks westward right quickly.

So, there we went, prancing blithely along, kicking up a little dust despite the mostly rocky trail. The mountains loomed behind us as we traversed the foothills defined by the North Platte River. There were stands of pine, but it was the cottonwood, willow, and aspen with their fresh green leaves that caught my appreciative eyes. The trail was well-worn, and I figured to enjoy it while I could. There were a couple of spots where wagon ruts had been captured for eternity in the limestone.

As I approached the spot from which the shooter had fired, I noted that he'd chosen well. There were plenty of spots from which a hidden marksman could dry-gulch an unsuspecting victim. I reminded myself to be wary of these spots as I tracked my prey. With a day's head start and any cursory checking of his back trail, he'd know that he hadn't been followed. Would he think he was safe and grow careless?

I found the cottonwood where he'd kneeled and climbed from Mukue's saddle. The grass was still trampled down from his knee and foot. There was a handy notch on the side of the tree trunk that would have been perfect to set the barrel of his rifle. Sure enough, the bark within the notch had been bruised. I looked around and quickly found a couple of shell casings. By that, I confirmed my suspicion that he was careless. He'd used a Winchester rifle, by my best guess. I watched Taabe as he excitedly sniffed around the place where the man had kneeled. "What's up, Taabe?" He seemed anxious to follow the shooter.

Now, my inbred Comanche tracking skills were ready to kick in. I found the hoofprints of the shooter's horse. There was something vaguely familiar about them. It was shod, but the shoe on the right leg was chipped. Since I was caught up in the business of horses,

I tended to notice distinguishing features like this. Where had I seen it?

The man's head start troubled me a might. I kept reminding myself to not be careless. He likely ran off a good distance but would have slowed down once he realized he wasn't immediately followed. I tried to get into the shooter's head. Why had he shot at us? If I could figure his motive, it would give me considerable insight into what drove his behavior. He apparently mounted up right quickly after his second shot at us, as the heel prints in the soil were deep and the strides long. He'd ridden off at a gallop. Having found no further sign and with Taabe anxious, I mounted up and followed the horse's tracks.

Before long, the tracks turned into the North Platte River. He must have had a time of crossing, as the snow-fed waters were running wild. As I looked up and down the river; however, this was as good a place as any to cross. If he was headed north, he was headed into country I knew like the back of my hand.

I managed to hold my gear high enough to make it across the river without soaking anything important. Taabe quickly picked up the trail. He wanted to run, but I kept a slower, steady pace, ever alert to possible ambush. The tracks were only a day old and easy to follow. My prey was making no effort to hide his trail. Still, I reckoned that he could be fifteen or more miles ahead of me. I had not yet figured out whether he had some destination in mind.

Where would a man run off to after trying to dry-gulch somebody? That brought me back to wondering whom he was targeting. He'd narrowly missed Cutter, but was he the target? Was it someone with designs on Esmeralda who was jealous? Was he simply a terrible marksman? These thoughts gnawed at me like a wolf to its prey. Now, there was an image. Taabe had been excited. Was the shooter someone Taabe had encountered? There weren't many who survived a wolf attack.

The trees were casting ever-longer shadows as the sun began to sneak behind the mountains to my west. I figured that whomever I was tracking was far enough ahead that I could afford a small fire. A little coffee would be pleasurable. I unsaddled Mukue and picketed him near some lush grass. He was close enough that he and Taabe would serve as my warning sentries should any threat approach.

I admit to enjoying the sights and sounds of the night. They tended to give my soul peace. In the twilight, I spotted a great horned owl dive for its prey. Like me, the hunters enjoyed the night. The shadows afforded them cover in stalking their victims.

The vastness of the night sky with millions of twinkling stars captured my heart and soul, no matter how many nights I slept beneath them. There was a timelessness about it all. I built a small fire and began heating the coffee. The crackle of burning sticks contrasted with the chirps and howls of the forest shrouded in the night. I found myself mesmerized by the flames licking the sides of the coffee pot as I chewed on some jerky and savored the last of that delicious bear sign goodie. About the only thing I missed was Morning Star.

I heard a bit of a scuffle a short distance off. Taabe had found his dinner.

Soon enough, I found myself yawning and curled up in my blanket with Taabe nestled beside me.

* * *

I awakened in the grayness of early morning. The sun was about to peek over the forested hills to my east. I stood and shook myself awake. I stirred what remained of the coals from last night's fire and warmed what remained of the coffee. While that heated, I put on my hat and then my moccasins. Oh, I wore moccasins because they offered stealth in the event that I had to sneak up on my prey. I buckled on my gun belt, then knelt by the fire and sipped the last of the coffee. Taabe pranced around, anxious as ever to resume the hunt.

I stamped out the fire and swept the area of evidence of my presence, as I'd learned long ago to never leave a trace of having been at a campsite. It preserved the pristine nature of the land and hid your having been there from friend or foe. I saddled Mukue and mounted up.

Taabe picked up the trail before I could, and we proceeded at an easy walk. About an hour into our day, we came upon the spot where the shooter had camped. Taabe got especially excited at discovering a piece of cloth. I climbed from my saddle for a closer inspection. The cloth was stained a dark brown from what looked to be dried blood. Now, things were beginning to come together. The clues were telling me that this was one of the men who'd tried to attack me at the ranch a few days back. Taabe had torn the man's arm enough to break it.

This piece of cloth was likely from the splint I'd fashioned. His marksmanship was off because he had trouble shooting the rifle. His desire for revenge at embarrassing him and his companions had apparently overridden his desire to accompany them with the wagon train. Now, I recognized the damaged horseshoe from one of the men's horses. It was all coming together. Once embedded in men's minds, revenge could drive them to dry-gulch. It was the coward's way.

"Good job, Taabe," I said with a ruffle of his shaggy neck. For his part, he was anxious to get back on the trail.

We now knew whom we were pursuing. The fact that our prey was driven by revenge and its all-encompassing sense of hatred meant that we must be extra careful. Hate tended to make folks not think straight, so there was no telling what he might be up to. He might even assume I'd be tracking him and set an ambush.

CHAPTER 13

NOT SO EASY

My Comanche intuition told me that Granger's wounded condition would lead him to follow the easiest trail. Despite the condition in which he'd left his campsite, his failure to hide his trail, and his state of mind, I dared not underestimate the man. He might not be a sharpshooter, but he could get lucky. I reasoned that he expected me to be following his tracks.

He was making the tracking too easy, as he took an old deer trail that led up the slope of the northern end of the Laramie Mountains. I'd traveled that trail a half dozen times and knew where just about every nook and cranny was. Problem was that there were a lot of hiding places that were ideal for an ambush. If his lame-brain idea had been to lure me in, he'd succeeded. However, as I'd heard a cowpoke or two say, *this wasn't my first rodeo*.

Mukue, Taabe, and I had been poking along cautiously for the better part of the day when we came upon another campsite. Hoofprints around the site confirmed that Granger had been there. Importantly, the coals he'd left behind were warm to the touch. I judged him to be no more than a couple of hours ahead of me. I'd just about reached the conclusion that he had no idea where he was headed when he reached a fork in the trail and his tracks took him southward. What could he have in mind now? Whatever it was, he was up to no good.

I was well-acquainted with this spot on the deer trail and knew that the trail to the right looped around and merged back in about three miles ahead. If Granger was going to lie for me anywhere nearby, he wouldn't be expecting me to have circled behind him.

It was getting to be late afternoon. I got to thinking that the sun would set in about three hours. Patience was the order of the day, so I dismounted. There was plenty of lodgepole pine standing between me and wherever Granger was. Assuming he'd soon stop for the night, I found a seat on a nearby log and waited for him to build a campfire so I could pinpoint his location.

I waited. And I waited. I kept telling myself to be patient. Dusk was settling in. Where was Granger's campfire?

I eventually fell asleep. I awakened not long after midnight. Peering into the trees, I saw no sign of flames. Had he cold camped? Mukue and Taabe were relaxed. The sounds of the night serenaded us uninterrupted. Had I underestimated him?

Come first light, I headed off-trail in the direction of the trail Granger had taken. It didn't take long to reach the trail and find his tracks. Those led us to a spot where he must have rested just long enough to leave a note. I now wondered as to what God was leading me into. What sort of test lay ahead? He'd given me choices, but was I making the right ones?

The note was simple. Capital letters simply said, "YOU MISSED ME." Well, it seemed that I had indeed underestimated Granger. He now saw fit to tease me. Any advantage I'd been enjoying was lost. Instead of hunter versus prey, it had become hunter versus hunter. To add to my frustration, clouds were rolling in. It was fixing to rain.

There was no point in getting too close to Granger, so I let him build a bit of distance between us. So long as it was going to rain, I set up my slicker between a couple of pine trees and hunkered down with Taabe by my side. Poor Mukue would have to endure a cool spring shower beneath what little shelter the pine boughs offered.

I sat pondering my situation. A chipmunk ran up the barrel of my Marlin and leaped out into the forest just as the first raindrops fell. I lamented that my guns and bow and arrows sure were no good with no prey to shoot at. Still, I figured I was in pretty fair shape here beneath a tree so long as some varmint like a bobcat or rattler wasn't looking to share a dry shelter.

Why was Granger heading south? He didn't have a prayer of catching up with his former companions, who were long gone on the trail to Oregon. What would draw him southward? Then, it hit me like a rifle butt slammed up the side of my head. He was heading for the Laramie Cross Breed Ranch. He'd lured me up here so he would be free to wreak havoc on my ranch with me not around.

* * *

It was tough to admit that I'd been taken in by a one-armed, dry-gulching, ne'er-do-well who held a deep-seated hatred for Indians. My pride was hurt. I'd just been injected with a dose of humility for having under-estimated my foe.

"Home!" I shouted as I leaped onto Mukue's saddle.

Taabe was off like a shot. There was no question that he was looking forward to getting another taste of John Granger. We careened down the trail at a full gallop for about a quarter mile before my better judgment took hold. If Granger was smart enough to lure me up here, he might figure I'd overreact and come blazing down the trail into an ambush.

The ground was still wet from the earlier rain, so my prey's tracks weren't hard to follow. He was riding at a near canter in his effort to put distance between us. I breathed deep and eased Mukue to a brisk walk while my eyes scanned the trees and rock outcroppings for any hint of Granger. The sun had finally emerged from the cloud cover and created myriad shadows along the trail.

We passed a huge grizzly cavorting with his mate about a hundred yards off the trail. He likely wouldn't have appreciated my grizzly claw necklace. Or would he have been impressed? I chuckled at the brief diversion. I found myself dealing with a touch of anxiety given my predicament, and the bear served to relieve it a tad.

It wasn't long before the North Platte River lay ahead. It was running wild with snow melt. Granger's tracks headed into what looked to be strong enough to qualify as rapids. There wasn't time to travel downstream to the wide shallow section that we'd crossed two days before. If Granger had crossed here, I had little choice. Then again, what if he was holed up on the south bank waiting to catch me in mid-stream? I'd be a sitting duck. Even if he missed, it could cause panic. I could be swept off Mukue and drown.

The possible outcomes weren't especially attractive. I saw nothing on the south bank but decided not to chance a crossing here. The waters downstream appeared especially rough, so I looked upstream where the river was flowing from the mountains and picking up little streams and creeks as it gathered momentum. Tumbling over rocks and fed by snow, it presented quite a challenge. While the angry waters were beautiful as they caught the colors of the trees, early blooms, and the crystal blue sky, they'd as soon been painted on the landscape by the Devil himself. Nevertheless, I turned westward to search for a crossing.

I was lucky. Or maybe God was looking out for me. About a quarter mile upstream, a couple of trees had fallen partway across the river. They created just enough of a logjam to back up and even calm the waters. The cowboy skills my pa had taught me, and I'd gotten to practice plenty of lassoing as I grew up on our ranch. My skill would now be put to the test. I lassoed a large branch of the bigger of the two trees on the first toss and secured the rope to Mukue.

After considerable urging, I managed to get Taabe draped over my saddle. I bundled everything as high as possible behind that saddle. We eased down the north bank and into the water with me clinging to Mukue's tail. It wasn't easy, but we were soon climbing from the chilly waters and on the south bank, enjoying the warming rays of the sun. It was tempting to immediately resume the chase, but the crossing had required considerable energy to accomplish. We all needed a rest. Besides, I needed to be sure that my guns and ammunition had stayed dry.

* * *

After our brief rest, we headed east to pick up Granger's trail. I looked around for sign upon reaching the place where he'd crossed. I found a spot where he'd knelt. No doubt he had figured to ambush me as I crossed the river. My decision to head west surely frustrated his plan. I mostly suppressed a smile at having outwitted him.

His trail headed directly toward my ranch. I wasn't sure what he expected there. If he chose to attack, he'd surely be committing suicide. I sure as shooting dared not underestimate him again.

CHAPTER 14

MERCY

We soon broke free of the tree line. Other than cottonwoods and willows growing along streams, only rolling prairie lay ahead. Somewhere ahead of us, Granger was planning some sort of revenge for my having embarrassed him. The combination of that and my being in his eyes a hated half-breed seemed to be enough to motivate him to take extreme measures.

I was confident that Morning Star could defend herself, and our ranch hands were fully capable of fighting off any threat. We'd all had experience fighting Indians. Why was I so worried about one physically handicapped man?

* * *

Granger boldly rode straight on up to the front of our house on the Laramie Cross Breed Ranch. Well, *boldly* might be an exaggeration. He likely spotted Morning Star peeking from the window. He pretended to be seriously hurting as he half fell from his saddle and staggered over to knock on the front door. As Morning Star unlatched the door and began to open it, his hand went to his gun. He thrust his foot into the threshold to block her from closing the door and put the muzzle of his revolver under her chin. "Just step back inside, squaw," he growled.

"What you want?" she demanded fearlessly.

Granger likely didn't expect the strength in her voice. He didn't realize that he was dealing with a woman who'd killed and scalped enemy warriors and had traveled the frontier and conquered its dangers. "Mebbe yuh don't understand, squaw. You stay quiet. We be waitin' fer yer half-breed husband," he snarled.

Michael began crying from his bed, and Morning Star struggled to get away from Granger's gun to tend to him.

"Don't pay the kid no mind," commanded Granger. "Yer breed man be along any time now. Let's greet his hide." Using his bad arm to pretend it held the gun to her back, he'd managed to holster his gun and grab a knife, which he now held at her back. He pushed her ahead of him through the front door.

* * *

Donovan, who was standing inside the nearby corral tending to a Quarter Horse, saw what was happening but held back for fear of the threat to Morning Star's life. To his right, he spotted me approaching with my bow and a nocked arrow hand.

What Donovan and Granger failed to see was Taabe stealthily sneaking to the side of the house just behind and to one side of his prey.

Donovan ducked low and headed for his house to fetch his rifle.

Granger hadn't noticed him. He had that knife tip drawing a bit of blood at Morning Star's back and focused his attention on my approach. He expected me to come over the high ground in front of our house and be facing him head-on.

* * *

I rode in slowly. Upon cresting that high ground in front of our house, the suspicions I'd had of Granger were fully confirmed. The expression on Morning Star's face communicated the desperation of her situation.

"Yuh stop thar an' git off thet hoss!" shouted Granger. "Do it now, or I be drivin' this here knife into yer wuthless squaw!"

I slipped from Mukue's saddle with my hands clear of my rifle and bow and arrows. The Colt still hung on my hip.

"What do you want, Granger?" I asked as calmly as I could manage.

"Nobody, 'specially no half-breed, be disrespectin' John Granger," he snarled. "I figger to let yuh see what I do to yer squaw afore I kill you." With that, his knife ripped upward through Morning Star's tunic, which fell open and exposed her.

I wanted to avert my eyes from my wife's embarrassment, yet stood frustrated that this fool with only one strong arm was such a threat. I urgently needed an opening to save her.

While Granger's attention had been focused on Morning Star and me, he failed to see Taabe stalking him. The wolf was but ten feet from him when a deep growl rumbled forth from him. Granger looked with horror at the bared fangs coming toward him. He fell away from Morning Star and swiped with his knife to no avail. Taabe leaped past and threw his better than a hundred and fifty pounds against Morning Star, shoving her to the ground. As he turned to attack Granger, my Colt had already spit lead. Granger's knife went flying, and my bullet rendered his good arm useless. A snarling Taabe stood atop him, spittle drooling into Granger's face.

"Back Taabe," I ordered as I went to Morning Star's side and covered her with the remains of her tunic.

Taabe wasn't attacking but was clearly reluctant to step away from Granger. His hot breath had Granger fully rattled.

With both arms disabled, Granger was fully at the mercy of the beast on top of him. He'd felt himself a big man, superior to any lowly Indian. He hadn't been able to see how short the shadow he cast was.

I strode over and gently pulled Taabe from Granger.

"H-h-he was gonna kill me," wailed Granger.

Morning Star had arisen and come to my side. "We kill and scalp?" She was half serious.

Fear was inadequate to describe the expression on Granger's face.

"No. He's helpless. It wouldn't be right to scalp him." I gazed down at the man groveling before me. "He deserves hanging," I stated matter-of-factly.

By now, Donovan had ambled on over with his Winchester in hand. "This the fellow shooting at us at the wedding?" he asked.

"Seems like," I replied. I shook my head resignedly. "Not much of a man," I added.

"Heard you mention hanging. I suppose it'd be legal."

The fear returned to Granger's eyes.

Morning Star and I exchanged glances. The time had come for mercy, an act that Granger would wholly not expect. While we held the power to punish him, we could also wield compassion in the form of forgiveness and kindness. I recalled my pa quoting Psalms, where it says something like, "The Lord is merciful and gracious, slow to anger, and abounding in steadfast love."

"Do you believe in God?" I asked Granger.

His eyes widened with incredulity, as though we were nuts. There he was, lying before us, vulnerable and in considerable pain, and we were asking him about his faith.

So far as I could make out, he lay there totally devoid of faith in a greater power. God hadn't yet graced the depths of his soul. George had shared some verses around the hearth at Christmas about how we should do nothing out of bitterness but humbly consider others as more important than ourselves. While we should look out for our own interests, we should also be concerned for the interests of others, regardless of their beliefs. He was applying that thinking to the Indians, but it sure worked here in consideration of Granger. I sure enough wanted to string him up to one of those cottonwoods out yonder, but something inside me said the man was worth another chance. "Well, John Granger, this is your lucky day."

"Wh-wh-what?" he whimpered.

"You think you're some sort of tough guy, and I understand that it can be as tough to admit that you've met your match. But the strength that resides within me comes from a higher power. Your hatred of Indians blinded you to greater truths."

Now, Granger's face changed quite markedly. He was

still in considerable pain, but—grudging as it might be—I'd grabbed his attention. Was his deep-seated prejudice still lurking? Of course, he was in no position to be bargaining.

Morning Star had headed back inside our home to replace her damaged clothing and to grab some medicinal materials as well. Bandages and poultices were in her arms as she re-emerged. She kneeled beside Granger and tore open the shirt covering where my bullet had passed clean through his shoulder. He flinched with pain. She examined the wound, then looked up at Donovan and me. "He go inside," she urged.

Granger couldn't bring himself to fully believe that we weren't going to scalp or hang him.

Donovan put aside his rifle to help me carry Granger inside. As we lifted him, he passed out, making it easier for us to lay him out on our kitchen table.

"Thanks, Chester," I said. "Please hang around. If he wakes up, we might need help holding him down."

Morning Star heated some water and soaked towels to wash Granger's wounds. She was intent on treating both the gunshot wound and the nasty-looking mess where Taabe had broken the arm and laid the flesh open. Since she didn't have to dig around for a bullet, the shoulder wound could be treated with poultices and a bandage. The broken arm was another matter. Infection had set in. The arm gave off a foul odor.

I thought back to how the Army surgeon had treated the terrible wounds from the bear's claws. The best we could do would be to clean out the infection as best possible, apply poultices, set the arm in a proper splint, and pray.

Once Morning Star finished her work on Granger's

wounds, we laid him out on a straw-filled tick and waited for him to wake up. I thanked Donovan and bade him return to his chores.

CHAPTER 15

CHANGED MAN

Upon awakening, Granger tilted his head up and looked about groggily. He slowly became aware that his wounds had been treated. Blinking a couple of times, he brought his eyes into focus on me sitting at the kitchen table, sipping coffee. He attempted to sit up but fell back. "Why yuh bein' good tuh me?" he muttered.

I gently placed my coffee cup on the table. "Killing you would have been easy, but it's not our way. We reckoned you were worth saving."

"B-b-but I…" His voice trailed off.

"Mr. Granger, I've found that folks sometimes misplace their minds. I don't know why you have it in for Indians, but you hold a misplaced hatred."

"Osage killed my ma," responded Granger.

"Sorry. My pa lost his folks to Comanche. He wound up forgiving them and marrying the sister of his best friend, a Comanche shaman. The sister is my ma." I paused and took a long sip of coffee. Morning Star eased over and refilled it.

"Are you hungry?" she asked Granger. "I have soup."

Granger nodded. "Kin I set at yer table?"

We lifted the man and set him gently at our table.

"I've fought Cheyenne and Kiowa, Mr. Granger. I scouted for Colonel Stanley on the Yellowstone Expedition. I've been bushwhacked, and I killed a grizzly hand-to-hand. It can be a tough life out here, but I've never lost the vision of God's gifting us with this majestic land He'd put us in charge of. My pa taught me that if we follow worthless things, we become worthless. We found that our trust in God has gifted us with the faith, courage, determination, and love to endure the toughest trials."

"Yuh don't hate me?" asked Granger as he awkwardly ladled soup into his mouth. "This be good soup, ma'am," he said distractedly.

I was encouraged that he'd referred to Morning Star as *ma'am* instead of *squaw*. "No, we neither hate nor fear you. Like I said, your mind was simply misplaced. Your ma's death affected your moral sanity. Emotion took over from your common sense and enslaved you."

Granger looked up at Morning Star. "Thanks fer treatin' my wounds." He turned to me. "What if—"

"I'd have killed you," I interjected.

"An' yuh would have done right," he admitted. "Thanks fer not doin' that."

It was going to be a warm day, so I decided to trade my buckskin shirt for one of lighter-weight cotton. As I stripped off my shirt, Granger couldn't miss the scars on my back and arms from the grizzly.

"Grizzly?" he asked.

"Critter had the spunk to wrestle me. He lost." I slipped on the cotton shirt.

"Don't be worryin' none. I ain't raslin' yuh." Granger managed to crack a smile.

"It's going to be a couple of weeks before you're trail worthy. We can put you up at the bunkhouse or cart you off to Fort Laramie."

Granger smiled. "I done my time with the Army. Kin I help any while I heal up?"

I nodded. "First, you must get strong enough to earn your keep. I'll get my partner to set you up in the bunkhouse. He'll find something for you to do that you'll be able to handle." I stood, then paused. "Do you read?"

Granger nodded. "A bit. Ain't done none fer a while."

"There are a couple of Bibles out in the bunkhouse. You might do some reading." With that, I went out to fetch Donovan and Moon to help Granger to the bunkhouse. I reckoned he was a changed man.

* * *

I finally found time to read *Ben Hur* and was glad I did. I found myself regretting not reading it sooner. It turned out to be the story of a fellow named Judah Ben Hur, a wealthy Jewish prince in 1st-century Jerusalem. He is betrayed by his childhood friend Messala and enslaved by the Romans. Ben Hur saves the life of a Roman named Quintus Arrius, who trains him to be a charioteer. That chariot apparently was a two-wheeled contraption pulled by four horses and used for racing and in battle. They must have been scary as all get out and tough to control.

Ben Hur returns to Jerusalem to seek revenge against Messala but winds up witnessing the life and crucifixion of Christ, ultimately transforming his desire for vengeance into forgiveness and compassion. The story weaves in themes of betrayal, justice, faith, and redemption and culminates in Judah's transformation. It turned out to be impactful for me, as I found that Ben Hur's life paralleled some of my own, and especially my pa's.

When I wasn't reading over the next couple of weeks, we added a porch, or what we called a gallery, across the front of our house. It afforded a shady, restful vantage point to sit back and sip coffee while enjoying the view of the distant Laramie Mountains. So it was that as I sat there one morning reading, I looked up to watch an eagle floating on a thermal. I then caught sight of some grazing deer. It sure looked lovely. I savored a sip of coffee, closed the book, and stared out onto the vista before me. I found myself pondering our future.

I soon heard footsteps as Morning Star ventured out with Moses running along behind and Michael in her arms. "Mountains pretty. Still snow on top," she observed. "What Isa think about?" she asked as she leaned against the railing beside me and smiled.

"We have been given much. Cutter and Esmeralda are building a life nearby, Donovan and Pearl have a new baby, our Quarter Horses are in demand, the cattle ranch in Texas begs for my attention, our boys are growing, and I have a beautiful, loving wife." Truth be told, what had been given was the opportunity to build what we had. It had been up to us to bring it to fruition.

She blushed a little. "And?" she pressed, as she fiddled distractedly with an earring that Michael yearned to grab.

"Do you still want to see your people at Standing Rock?"

She smiled. "You do this for me?"

I looked up at her with a grin. "Who else?" I replied.

She nearly dropped young Michael as she hugged me. "Awentia very happy."

"Granger is about healed up," I said beneath her

breathtaking hugs and kisses. "He says that he wants to catch up with his friends headed to Oregon."

Morning Star was totally ignoring my remarks about Granger.

"He asked if he could keep the Bible." Whether the Bible would make a difference to Granger would depend on his inclination to read it and apply it.

She pressed closer.

I finally yielded to her embrace, and we staggered inside and fell onto the bearskin in front of the hearth. I hoped Moses and Michael would forget seeing what ensued.

CHAPTER 16

DECISIONS

Morning Star enthusiastically poured herself into preparations for our journey to the Standing Rock Agency. Formerly known as the Grand River Agency, established on the banks of said river in 1968, it was relocated upstream in 1874 and renamed the Standing Rock Agency. The governance of the agency was housed at Fort Yates, where Sitting Bull surrendered in 1881 after having to leave Canada.

We had serious decisions to make. The operations of Laramie Cross Breed Ranch had to continue, but the greater question was whether to bring Moses and Michael on so arduous a journey. Morning Star was intent on bringing supplies, but a wagon would bog us down considerably over the more than four-hundred-mile distance. We could do the trip in about two weeks using packhorses and pressing hard, whereas it would take better than a month by wagon. We also had to guess what sort of supplies the Lakota might need for the months ahead. We'd heard from troopers at Fort Laramie that the tribes at Standing Rock were not receiving their promised allotments. This was a common problem among the Indian agencies. My pa shared with me that the Comanche in Oklahoma experienced similar challenges and had to learn to fend for themselves.

Donovan would take responsibility for running ranch operations, with Cutter helping out some part-time, and Moon as full-time ranch hand. We'd offered Granger the opportunity to stay on, but he was set on joining his friends in Oregon. Donovan's wife, Pearl, offered to watch the boys while we traveled, but Morning Star was committed to tribal tradition. The entire family must travel together.

Indian hostilities were mostly at an end. Even the return of Sitting Bull last year had gone peacefully despite worries that he'd rile up the Sioux. The last conflict around the region had been with Chief Joseph and the Nez Percé, who were chased across more than a thousand miles of mountains by General Oliver Howard about five years ago. The Cheyenne and Arapaho were at peace. Far as I could tell, there should be no trouble.

On a visit to Fort Laramie, I learned from Captain Hayes that the Indian agent at the Standing Rock Agency was a fellow named James McLaughlin. The commander at Fort Yates was Major Charles Alden, an Army surgeon. He was a little out of his element, being thrust as he was among the Indians. McLaughlin and Townsend were apparently working on some agreement with the Sioux tribes to equitably apportion the reserva-tion per the Dawes Act, toward ensuring fair and adequate distribution of rations and annuities.

Fool Heart, Hump, and Circle Bear were the three chiefs heading the Miniconjou Lakota at Standing Rock. Hayes said that McLaughlin was formerly a blacksmith but had exhibited an ability to deal with the Indians and had eventually been given the Standing Rock assignment. He was intent on getting the Lakota to adopt subsistence-style farming and giving up their nomadic hunting lifestyle. However, Hayes assured me that local climate and geographic conditions made such agricultural pursuits difficult, as the land allotments given to the people proved to be too small.

Captain Hayes took me aside in confidence and shared that he'd heard that the rations and annuities didn't measure up to what had been agreed to. The Lakota were struggling to keep everyone fed.

Thus armed with what Hayes shared with us, we continued to prepare for the journey northward. The Standing Rock Agency encompassed the headwaters of the Grand River well north of Deadwood and Spearfish.

Of course, Moses was super excited as he sensed what lay ahead. He'd be getting to ride a horse, although he still needed the modified saddle. Michael was just barely walking, so he would travel in a rig mounted behind Morning Star on Spirit Horse. We had a string of four packhorses. One was for our personal gear and food, while the others would carry supplies for the Lakota people. What we brought for the people didn't seem like all that much, but I expected that every little bit would help. I was prayerfully cooking up a grander plan but wanted to see firsthand what we would be facing at Standing Rock. For now, coffee, tobacco, cornmeal, and a few blankets would have to suffice.

Folks never ventured out on the frontier wilds without sufficient weaponry. We were no exception. I was grateful that Morning Star was capable with a rifle as well as a bow and arrows. So it was that we carried our bows and arrows and our knives. I had my trusty Colt Peacemaker in its holster on my hip. We completed our armament with Morning Star's Winchester, my Marlin, and my Spencer, carried in scabbards on either side of my saddle. Naturally, we had plenty of ammunition and expected to add more as needed in Rapid City or Deadwood.

* * *

We departed on a crystal-clear day in early June. I expect that we looked to be quite a sight. I was of a mind to pick up the Western Trail that the cattle drives were following into Canada. I figured that it would be easier going than cutting our own trail. There'd be plenty of watering holes for us and our livestock, as well as stream-fed grasses.

I figured to follow a branch of the Western Cattle Trail that followed the natural valleys well east of the Bighorn Mountains. That route would bring us to Rapid City, just south of Deadwood. To my surprise, we happened upon the Cheyenne to Deadwood stagecoach road. I was apprehensive about following it but reckoned it would speed our travels a tad.

We fell into a daily routine. My aim was to cover about twenty-five miles each day, depending on the road condition. We'd camp just before sunset. Each of us, including Moses, had assigned tasks. I cared for the livestock and built a cooking fire, while Morning Star tended to the cooking and baby Michael. Moses' duties were to gather firewood and lay out bedrolls. We'd eat, enjoy the fresh mountain air, sing a song or two, and turn in. I picketed the horses nearby so any threat that alerted them would awaken us. Taabe slept alongside Morning Star and me. Naturally, he tended to be alerted to threats sooner than the horses.

During the day, I led the way while Morning Star and Moses rode beside the tethered packhorses. We were constantly alert for humans and animals. Our past experiences with bears and similar hunters of the frontier made us especially sensitive to their presence. As it was, we saw four grizzlies and a mountain lion during the first four days. I was every bit as concerned with the dangers posed by humans. There were surely travelers who, like Granger and the fellow at The Emigrant's Washtub, held animosity toward Indians. A procession of a half dozen horses with plenty of trade goods aboard, guarded by a single man with a woman and small children, could pose a tempting attraction for troublemakers.

The landscape was breathtaking, and we had plenty of time to enjoy it. Calling the country beautiful didn't do it justice. We found ourselves marveling as bald eagles floated high above us, then perched on the limbs of cottonwoods that gave them a great vantage point to look for prey. The air was filled with the fragrance of sagebrush and wildflowers like primrose, larkspur, wild rose, and paintbrush. The landscape was downright gawdy with color as though God had swept a great paintbrush across it.

At night, we could hear the occasional flutter of the great horned owl's wings as it lifted off with its tiny prey. Taabe would come alert at the distant sounds of wolves or coyotes. The nights were clear, and the stars bright and plentiful. It was mostly so quiet that you could hear the stars twinkle at night. Now and then, a bull elk would make its bugling call.

This was country that had been fought over. Much blood had been shed. The Osage had pushed the Comanche south. The Comanche took Apache lands and set up a vast trading empire. At various times, the various bands of Lakota were both friends and enemies. The Crow defended their lands from encroaching Sioux. Then, the White men came, ignored treaties, and took the lands from Indians who had no idea as to the concept of land ownership. Even among the White settlers, there was constant turnover of ownership.

The Indians had now been confined on well-defined tracts, yet even the twenty-two million acres of the Standing Rock Agency were insufficient to sustain the tribes. The vast herds of buffalo were disappearing, and the young men and women were losing the traditional roles passed from generation to generation. The largesse of the White man's government had caused them to be dependent for food and shelter.

* * *

Thus far, we had encountered no fellow travelers. A couple of times, we spotted smoke from distant cabins. The way the frontier was being settled, I had expected to encounter folks. I was on the lookout for the dust raising that gave evidence of a cattle drive. We'd left the stage-coach road as I sought a more direct route to Fort Yates.

On the fifth night, I found myself unable to sleep. Something was on my mind, gnawing at me. It was as though my senses were warning me. Try as I might, I struggled to identify the threat.

I felt Taabe's nose nudge me. Did he sense something, too? He laid his head upon my chest, his big blue eyes gazing at me as though trying to communicate.

"What is it?" I whispered.

Careful so as to not disturb Morning Star or our boys, I slipped on my moccasins and stood.

Taabe headed off to a nearby bluff and stood with head high. He lifted his nose as though seeking to capture a scent.

I strode over and stood beside him. The stars and moon cast a dim whiteness over the countryside before us. I saw nothing.

Taabe even seemed bewildered as his nostrils flared with whatever scent he'd captured. He wasn't acting concerned, as he might were a threat to be nearby. Something wasn't quite adding up, and neither of us could figure it out. The hairs on the back of my neck were still standing on end a bit, but whatever was causing my discomfort wasn't obvious.

Shrugging, I finally turned and headed back toward my bedroll. I looked up to see that our fire had been rekindled. Alarmed, I quickened my pace with Taabe trotting silently along beside me. The fact that he wasn't growling barely lessened my concern.

Morning Star was sitting upright while somebody stoked the flames. From what I could see of her as the fire cast its flickering light, she appeared calm and collected.

I soon made out the form of a man. In a low voice so as to not wake the children, I asked, "Who are you?" The light of the fire showed him to be a white-haired old man. He looked to be a White man and dressed not unlike our mountain man friend Wally.

"Howdy," he replied in a near whisper. "Just met yer fine wife, Awentia. Yuh must be Isa. I be Mountain Jack Floyd."

I shook my head a bit, as I didn't know quite what to make of this situation. "What are you doing here in the middle of the night?" I asked, again keeping my voice down.

Mountain Jack poked at the fire with a stick. Off behind him stood his mule, a rather sturdy-looking beast packed with furs and the supplies of a well-traveled man. "The mule be Sally," he said in answer to my unspoken question. "I be here 'cause I been followin' the Crow followin' y'all fer two days now."

"Why stoke the fire?" I pressed him. Why on earth was he of a mind to make it easier for the Crow to see us?

"Shucks, Isa. They already know yer here." He assured me.

Mountain Jack was right. There was no point in any attempt to hide our existence. "Aren't the Crow at peace?"

He offered a nearly toothless smile. "Not this bunch. Band of hotheads. Mebbe seven of them savages. Want yer hosses they do."

Morning Star and I exchanged concerned looks. We looked over and were satisfied that Moses and Michael were still asleep.

"There were nine," shared Mountain Jack, as he held two bloody scalps aloft. He smiled at our not reacting to the grisly scalps. "Y'all good with them bows an' arrows?" he asked.

We nodded.

His eyes grew wide. "Better grab'em!" he warned, as he tossed a blanket over the campfire to snuff the flames. "They be comin'!"

Our eyes quickly adjusted to the darkness.

I strung our bows right quickly and handed one to Morning Star. She'd already retrieved our arrow-filled quivers and tossed mine to me.

Mountain Jack had his own bow and arrows at the ready and had already nocked an arrow as he made a hand signal to head to his left while he went to the right. "They be comin' from yonder," he advised with a nod of his head. "We git 'em in a crossfire." He was still whispering, but with intensity.

Morning Star and I nocked arrows and waited for the inevitable attack.

* * *

The first Crow warrior came charging directly toward me on his war pony. I caught the reflection of the feathers in his horse's mane and on his bone breastplate. He was nearly on top of me when I released my first arrow. The shaft traveled through the pony's neck and into the savage's throat. His pony was already falling as they tumbled past.

Meanwhile, Morning Star had sent an arrow through a club-wielding Crow's side, severely wounding him. He rode past and pivoted his pony for another charge. With an arrow sticking from his ribs, he managed to raise the war club high. It was enough for her second arrow to finish him.

From the corner of my eye, I saw Mountain Jack fire an arrow clean through a warrior's chest. The savage rode on but was dead in his saddle. I turned back to the sound of another war pony coming straight at me. My arrow went wild, and the Crow hostile leaped from his pony with knife in hand. His momentum knocked me to the ground, but I was able to roll away. He was a picture of pure hatred and wildness as he gripped his knife, ready for hand-to-hand battle.

Without question, he was of a mind to kill me. He was too close for my arrow, so I grabbed my Bowie knife. It was twice the size of his knife, but his was every bit as deadly. While I had a considerable physical advantage, he was a wiry savage and quick on his feet. He waved his knife at me as he tried to find a weakness in my defense.

I slipped on a rock. As I began to fall backward, my knife fell from my hand. The Crow saw his chance and jumped forward at me. He was about to pounce when one of Morning Star's arrows found its mark in the center of his chest.

The remaining Crow had by now been persuaded that theirs was a losing cause. The four remaining hostiles were soon galloping off in full retreat. So far as I could tell, two of them were wounded. They'd not soon be forgetting the trap they'd rode into.

I saw Morning Star close by. She had another arrow nocked and was scanning the darkness of the surrounding foliage.

Mountain Jack strode over. "Y'all okay here?" he whispered.

"They're gone," I noted with confidence.

Mountain Jack nodded. "Foolish young'uns," he observed. He motioned to Moses and Michael. "They be sleepin'," he said with a chuckle.

Morning Star walked over to the boys. They were sound asleep.

"Y'all done good. If y'all don't be mindin' it, I be obliged to park my body o'er yonder an' sleep some." He unstrung his bow and walked over to Sally. The mule had stood patiently while the battle raged around. In that respect, he was as good as our Mukue and Spirit Horse.

Before we could respond, he was unpacking his mule and laying out his bedroll under a nearby cottonwood tree.

* * *

Come morning, a shard of sunlight played on my face. I stood and surveilled our campsite. Mountain Jack and Sally were gone.

Moses and Michael stirred as I took another scan of our surroundings. The bodies of the Crow were gone or at least out of sight. I didn't reckon that the tattered remnants of the war party had retrieved them, so I deduced that Mountain Jack had dragged them out of sight.

As the boys rallied, Morning Star awakened to tend to them. We shared knowing smiles, as our young ones had been spared the brief but intense battle.

I was finishing my coffee as we prepared to depart when Moses came running. "Look, Pa!" he announced with one of Mountain Jack's arrows in hand.

"Where'd that come from?" I asked innocently.

"Moses find. Man sleep," he told me, and led me over to where one of the Crow savages lay behind some sagebrush.

"Shhh!" I warned. "Let him sleep. We go." We tiptoed away together. We dared not say he was dead.

Morning Star had watched us and smiled with amusement. "Man in deep sleep," she said jokingly.

"That was too close for comfort," I noted, as I cinched Mukue's saddle.

"Sleeping Crow or battle?" Morning Star was still in a humorous mood.

"Awentia in good spirits," I observed.

"Last night good," she replied. It confirmed the warrior that yet resided within the heart and soul of my Lakota wife. It was as though she reveled in the fight. I expected that I should be relieved that she didn't take a scalp. "Thankful for Mountain Jack," she added.

I did wonder where Mountain Jack had disappeared to. I'd hoped to ask him whether he knew Wally. I sighed wistfully. The chances of encountering him again were slim to none, as the frontier was so vast.

We were soon mounted up. With the Crow threat eliminated, we continued our journey.

CHAPTER 17

HOMESTRETCH

We made it to Rapid City in a breathtaking eleven days. We encountered no more threats to life and limb. We even passed a mile or so to the east of a rather large cattle drive that stretched out for several miles. In a few more days, we figured to be arriving at Fort Yates.

The boys were decidedly trail-weary. Riding up through the muddy main street of Rapid City, I wasn't especially impressed. Many of the buildings bore false fronts. The place had been established by gold miners who'd not been successful at Deadwood. The Black Hills had drawn like moths to a flame, men seeking riches. We figured to replenish our supplies and leave quickly, as we dared not be swept up in the skullduggery and mayhem of the town. Keeping in mind that these towns were built on lands that belonged to my ancestors by the Treaty of Fort Laramie in 1968, and us being Indians, we didn't feature on lingering.

"Ugly place," muttered Morning Star as we rode up to what served as a general store.

I nodded. There were a couple of shady-looking

characters hanging out on the boardwalk that ran across the front of the store, and I didn't think it wise to verbally insult their town. I dismounted and sidled over to Morning Star, still sitting her saddle. I slipped her rifle from its scabbard and placed it butt first across her lap. "If any trouble, shoot first," I warned.

She nodded knowingly to me as she pointed the muzzle of the Winchester in the general direction of the three unkempt men loitering beside the store. They looked to be up to no good.

With my hand on the butt of my Colt Peacemaker, I strode up the step to the boardwalk and into the store. Taabe followed me.

"Howdy," I said by way of greeting the store clerk. "I need ammunition and coffee. Could use some jerky, too, if y'all have any."

"You a breed, ain't yuh?" inquired the clerk edgily.

"That a problem?" I replied. "Think of it as the White part of me spending US coin here in your fine establishment."

He gave me a confused look as though trying to figure out what I'd said. "That a dog?" he asked.

"Timber wolf. He'll eat you as soon as look at you."

"Yer payin' cash money?" he said by way of reinforcement.

What had I just said? He obviously wasn't the brightest candle in Rapid City.

"Ammo?" he asked.

".44 caliber," I answered.

"Venison, elk, or beef jerky?" he continued.

"Little of each," I responded.

He placed the ammunition and jerky in a sack along with a bag of coffee. He cast a guarded look at Taabe. "Thet'll be four dollars."

"I'll take a couple sticks of yonder candy, too."

He tossed the candy into the bag. If he thought I'd argue over his prices, he was mistaken.

I paid him with silver and departed. Taabe preceded me out the doorway, pausing briefly to look at the three men. As I strode onto the boardwalk, one of the men stuck his foot out with the intention of tripping me. Fortunately, I'd been alerted by Taabe and was too sure-footed to fall for that trick. I swept my free hand low and caught the man's boot heel. With a yank, I sat his posterior with a thud on the boardwalk. The look of shock on the man's face was almost comical.

The man's companions stood back with gasps. Not a word had yet been spoken.

Ignoring them, I went over and tied the sack to our lead packhorse, then handed Moses a stick of candy.

"Yuh Injuns eat candy?" chided the man whom I'd tripped up. He managed to stand up from his embarrassing position.

I already knew that I was dealing with a bully. I could smell a bit of liquor on his breath, which likely contributed to his being bold enough to make trouble with a stranger who had him by fifty pounds and a few inches in height. "Yep. We enjoy the same food as y'all," I said, friendly-like. I didn't want trouble, especially in front of Moses.

The man had fully gathered himself and now stood about five feet from me. "I hate Injuns," he snarled. I'd discomfited him, and he was looking to save face. His hand dipped toward the grip on his revolver.

In a flash, the tip of my Bowie knife was under his chin. His hand eased back from his gun. I called over my shoulder. "Sweetheart, do we need any more scalps?"

The man's mouth gaped. His friends were frozen in place.

"No need scalp today," responded Morning Star. "Have plenty," she added, as she struggled to contain a smile despite the touchy situation.

"I didn't think so." I laid a steely gaze on the man. "Maybe Taabe here would like a taste."

The man had begun to tremble.

"Y'all are lucky that he's already eaten." I had an urge to run my Bowie knife clean through his chin up to the hilt and into his warped brain. I took a deep breath to settle myself. "Now, my family is going to ride on out of your fine little town, and you're not going to move a muscle until we're out of sight. Is that clear?"

The man nodded.

By now, a couple of more folks had been drawn to the confrontation. "Ride on out, sweetheart. I'll catch up shortly." I continued holding the knife at the man's chin until Morning Star had led our caravan out of sight.

The bully was now sweating profusely. He dared not move a muscle.

I deftly removed the man's gun from its holster and tossed it. I looked at his companions standing helplessly nearby. "Toss your guns over with his," I directed. The point of my knife accidentally pricked the bully's chin. He flinched but didn't move away. "Dang, now you've gotten blood on my knife," I scolded.

"S-s-sorry," he managed to get out. I glanced down and saw that he'd soiled his pants.

The men wasted no time obeying me, as their guns took wing. "Now, I'm sure y'all are fine upstanding citizens of Rapid City." I smiled. "The folks gathered here are surely glad y'all made no trouble. No telling where a missed bullet might land. Let's keep the town trouble-free."

"Yer pretty bold with thet knife at my chin," muttered the bully, as he tried to recover his manhood.

"Don't be getting persnickety," I admonished.

A bead of sweat trickled down his cheek.

With a sigh, I drew my Colt, shoved into the bully's belly, and slid my Bowie knife back into its sheath. "I'm even bolder with this," I said and pressed the muzzle hard into his gut. "And consider yourself lucky."

"Lucky?" he growled.

"My wife can shoot the eye out of a squirrel at fifty yards with that Winchester," I warned. "And she's taken scalps," I added with a tough-as-nails gaze. Still holding my gun on the bully and keeping my eye on the three men, I moved toward Mukue and climbed into the saddle. "You fellows don't move a muscle until I'm long gone. Is that understood?"

The three nodded vigorously.

I rode off with nary a look back over my shoulder. I imagined the three of them were beside themselves with indecision over whether to take the chance of going for their guns. I counted on them not being so stupid as to try. I had no desire to cause a ruckus by killing drunken men, whether justified or not.

* * *

The trail from Rapid City was best described as arduous. The hills and valleys, creeks, and many turns of our trail slowed us some. The terrain was tough on our horses. There was no telling what to expect on the convoluted game trails that we followed. Whether ascending or descending steep trails, switchbacks were common.

I encouraged Moses and must admit that he did well despite his modified saddle that made it difficult to use his heels to help guide his horse. To be straight, he was fast becoming quite a little horseman. He was growing, too. In a mere four years, I'd be teaching him the rifle and bow and arrows.

As we rode northeast from Rapid City, we watched for Indians. We'd been on the Great Sioux Reservation since leaving Wyoming, but now we were approaching the Standing Rock Agency and would be more likely to come upon roving bands of Indians—or vice versa.

It took us a day to reach and traverse the rushing waters of the Belle Fourche. We camped on the north bank. By now, we were wed to well-practiced routine. We had become downright proficient and setting and striking camp.

We hadn't talked about the incident back in Rapid City, and we skirted wide of Deadwood for fear of encountering a similar situation.

* * *

In addition to answering Morning Star's fervent desire to help the Miniconjou Lakota, the journey was giving us time to ourselves without the day-to-day interruptions of ranch life. We'd brought the Laramie Cross Breed Ranch to the point where it was going strongly enough to enable us to escape on this journey. I was proud of the way she rode, straight and fearless-looking. I'd been blessed with a strikingly beautiful wife, though it was her spirit that captivated me more than her physical appearance. In the time we'd been together, we'd endured life-threatening challenges but celebrated many wonderful experiences.

"Men at Rapid City drink too much," observed Morning Star out of the clear view, as we negotiated a switchback in the trail such that we faced each other.

I was so surprised that I failed to respond. Another switchback loomed ahead.

"Isa agree?" she asked.

"Liquor can make men do bad things." I pulled up, as did she. "The men hated our people, and the liquor revealed the hatred."

"Cattlemen in Cheyenne same," she said. Apparently, she'd been thinking about prejudice for quite a while.

"They are, but money can overcome prejudice."

Morning Star shook her head, then nudged Spirit Horse along.

I was left wondering what her negative reaction meant. Fortunately, we stopped for a rest a few minutes later. While the horses drank from a nearby creek and grazed on some lush grass, I reopened our brief conversation. "Do you not believe money overcomes prejudice?"

She gazed at me as though the answer was obvious. "They still hold hate inside. Money no matter. They afraid to lose money." She was right. As with Granger back at our ranch, it was necessary to root out the cause of prejudice. Hate was like a festering infection.

"So they hide their hatred behind smiles as they take our money," I said.

"When you have nothing more that they want, they show hate." Morning Star was right.

"Comanche traders did the same with Whites. When White man had plenty of trade goods, the Comanche would put aside their hate. When no trade goods, they killed." I looked to our west as the shadows lengthened across the landscape. Next day, we'd reach the headwaters of the Moreau and then travel on to Lake Oahe and Fort Yates.

Moses had already sprung into action, gathering kindling for our campfire. "What Ma and Pa say?"

Morning Star and I broke into laughter. He'd never previously expressed interest in our conversations, and he likely hadn't grasped what we were discussing. "We talk about people."

He responded with a curious look accentuated by a cock of his head.

"Some people do silly things for bad reasons," I said in an attempt to simplify a complicated concept.

"Moses need to meet other children," observed Morning Star. She was right about that, as he had only dealt with adults out here on the frontier. The only other children close by our ranch were his younger brother Michael, who was just beginning to talk, and the Donovans' newborn baby.

"I'll take him with me to Fort Laramie more often," I said by way of commitment.

CHAPTER 18

STANDING ROCK AGENCY

Fort Yates sat on a spit of land on Lake Oahe that was more island than peninsula. The lake was fed by the Grand River from the west. The Miniconjou Lakota had settled along its shores. The fort was more sprawling village than military post, as it lacked the traditional walls folks who'd never been out west expected to see. It had been little more than a year before our arrival that Tatanka Iyotake, known as Sitting Bull, had surrendered at Fort Yates. The place held a certain mysticism by virtue of the great medicine man and chief having spent time there.

As we turned to ride into the fort, I was taken by how depressed it seemed. The Indians especially appeared downtrodden. I reckoned to find McLaughlin, the Indian agent, before we headed for the Miniconjou encampment.

"Where you hail from?" asked a young corporal.

"Visiting from Fort Laramie way," I replied.

"There ain' no room fer more Injuns here," he advised. "Ate the last of the rations last week," he added. I detected a bit of regret in his voice. That said, he didn't appear to be starving.

"Where can we find Jim McLaughlin?"

"Yuh got agency business?" asked the corporal.

I found myself put off by the self-importance of the corporal. "We're here to see Circle Bear but wish to see McLaughlin first."

"Yuh be one of them breeds?" He smirked. He cast a leering eye at Morning Star. "Nice squaw," he remarked.

I was feeling a bit hot over the corporal's impertinence and prejudice. I gave him a hard look and raised an eyebrow. "She'd as soon scalp you as look at you, Corporal," I stated. "Then again, I'm pretty handy with a knife."

The corporal took a gander at the collection of weapons we carried. "Agent McLaughlin be o'er at yonder building," he said with a hard swallow while pointing to a tan structure that looked as though it had seen better days.

"Thanks, Corporal," I said and nudged Mukue toward the place pointed out by the corporal.

* * *

Our arrival did attract some attention, and I wasn't sure that all of it was friendly. The Lakota hanging around the fort premises looked yearningly at our packhorses. Many looked as though they hadn't eaten a square meal in days. "You stay here," I told Morning Star. "If anyone goes after our packhorses, shoot them." This would sound bold and even unfair to some folks, but such was the brutal reality of our situation. Moreover, Morning Star would shoot to protect us and our property.

I dismounted and strode over to the front door of

McLaughlin's headquarters. I was about to knock when the door opened. Standing before me was a slender man with wavy dark hair. A full mustache grew atop his lips while a goatee-like beard dangled from his chin. "Howdy, my name is Jim McLaughlin. May I help you folks? We've got space up in those hills yonder, but rations are lean."

I suspected the Indian rations were lean because the garrison was fattening up on what wasn't being sold for a tidy profit. "I'm Isa O'Toole. We bring gifts for Circle Bear."

McLaughlin stared at me as though I looked familiar. "You ride with Custer on the Yellowstone Expedition?"

"I scouted for Colonel Stanley," I replied. "Shame what happened to the 7th Cavalry."

That set well with McLaughlin. "Yep. A lot of good men took arrows that day." He looked at me, then over at Morning Star. "You Lakota?" he asked.

"I'm part Comanche. My wife is Miniconjou."

McLaughlin nodded. "Your pa White?"

"Yes." I found myself annoyed at constantly encountering folks worried about race. I was a human, and that should have been plenty.

"You be heading back to Fort Laramie?" He seemed to be wanting assurance that we wouldn't be staying on at Standing Rock Agency.

"I have a ranch to run."

"Cattle?" he asked.

"Quarter Horses," I replied.

"You ever get up this way again, I'd sure love a fine Quarter Horse." He looked away thoughtfully.

I didn't reckon that McLaughlin could afford one of my cayuses. "We just wanted to do you the courtesy of letting you know that we were here. I understand that the Miniconjou camp is west of here on the Grand River."

McLaughlin gazed up at the afternoon sun. "You likely have time to reach Circle Bear before nightfall." He took another look at our packhorses. "You'll be *very* welcome."

There was a touch of sarcasm in McLaughlin's opinion with its emphasis on *very*. It was obvious that he didn't want us hanging around Fort Yates, and I felt as though he wasn't being totally forthcoming about the Indians at the Standing Rock Agency. So far as I was concerned, I didn't feature having to stay up all night guarding our horses and supplies. "Thanks kindly, Mr. McLaughlin," I said and walked back to Mukue. I wanted to get away from Fort Yates as soon as possible.

* * *

We were intent on finding Circle Bear, one of the chiefs of the Miniconjou Lakota. We simply followed the well-worn trail along the south bank of the Grand River. As we rounded a gently bend, I spotted an Indian encampment about a half mile ahead. The sun would sink below the hills ahead of us in about an hour, so we pushed our horses a bit.

"We see Circle Bear and Hump," announced Morning Star enthusiastically.

I was a bit less optimistic. I didn't see the amount of smoke that would accompany a large camp. As we drew near, I spotted nine teepees. I was horrified. This was perhaps a quarter of what we expected. I reined Mukue in so Morning Star could come alongside. "Camp is small," I observed with a bit of distress.

Morning Star tried to contain her distress. "Not good. Hope Circle Bear well," she said.

"We will be welcome," I said, thinking back on McLaughlin's comment.

Moses rode up beside us. "Where Lakota?" He was referring to children. Sadly, there were no youngsters frolicking about the camp.

"Let's go," I said. "Keep chins up and smile."

As we entered the camp, folks began emerging from teepees. I spotted a teepee that was more heavily decorated than the others and assumed it to belong to Circle Bear, so we headed for it.

Men, women, and a mere handful of children followed our procession. They stared more with desperation than amazement at the bounty on our packhorses.

We pulled up before what I presumed to be Circle Bear's teepee.

One of the warriors who'd walked beside us strode over and shook a gourd rattle beside the entrance. Silence hung heavily on the gathering.

Circle Bear finally emerged. He didn't look well. He gazed curiously at us as though we were some sort of apparition.

I pointed to myself. "Me Isa O'Toole." I motioned toward Morning Star. "This Awentia, daughter of Wapitiyu Okle."

At the mention of Spotted Elk's name, Circle Bear perked up, as did a couple of the men standing nearby. "Wapitiyu Okle *kola*." He signed that Spotted Elk had gone to the spirit world.

I pointed back to our packhorses. "*Wóiyokihi* to Miniconjou." I told the chief that we'd brought gifts for his people.

Morning Star also motioned toward our packhorses. "*Wówanyanke*," she said, inviting the tribe to eat.

Circle Bear's own smile revealed teeth likely lost to insufficient nutrition. "Isa and Awentia welcome."

I was pleased that the chief knew English, but I was intent on flaunting my Lakota a bit. "*Sukawaka wóiyokihi* Circle Bear." I told him that the packhorses were a gift to him.

By now, the Lakota women were swarming around the packhorses, while the men held back. Morning Star dismounted to assist in unloading and distributing.

I dismounted, helped Moses from his horse, and stood beside Circle Bear. I would have helped with the unloading, but the Lakota culture dictated that women did this sort of work.

"Isa not Lakota," observed Circle Bear.

I expect it was the way I wore my hair that gave away my heritage. "Isa White and Penateka Comanche. My mother was daughter of Chief Buffalo Hump."

"Wapitiyu Okle tell stories about Isa O'Toole. Isa save Awentia from Cheyenne." It was reassuring that the chief knew something about me and that it was good. He looked at me with admiration, then glanced at Taabe. "Wolf good spirit?" he asked.

I nodded and ruffled Taabe's neck.

Circle Bear smiled knowingly. "Is good. Come, we smoke."

"Taabe watch Moses," I said, hoping he understood. I dutifully followed Circle Bear into his teepee.

Once seated before the fire in the center of the teepee, the chief lit a pipe. He took a puff and handed it to me.

"Where Miniconjou people?" The question had been gnawing at me, so I simply had to ask. As I awaited his response, I noted that the woman preparing some sort of drink behind him flinched at my question.

A sadness swept over Circle Bear's face. "Young men unhappy. Leave camp. Many Miniconjou get sick and die. Some starve."

"Doesn't the agency supply your rations?" I asked.

"They more worry about Tatanka Iyotake. They fear him. Make him want to leave. They take him to Fort Randall."

So, McLaughlin held back on rations and supplies to encourage Sitting Bull to leave willingly. It seemed the height of perversity. Having taken a draw on the pipe, I handed it back to Circle Bear. "Circle Bear stays at Standing Rock?" I asked.

"Old. No fight."

I shook my head. Those three words told me everything. The situation at Standing Rock Agency was sad, but sadder still was that the Lakota had given up. My pa had told me that if you teach a man to hunt deer; he will find them and not starve. If you give the man the deer, he will be ever dependent. This was like the government making the Lakota dependent on handouts. They had forgotten how to hunt for their own food. They had tried to turn the men into farmers, but that was counter to their culture, and most of the soil around the Standing Rock Agency didn't lend itself to planting food crops. Coupled with ever-fewer buffalo roaming the prairies, the situation for the Miniconjou and other Lakota people had grown desperate. "I can send more, but Miniconjou must help themselves." I accepted a drink from the woman.

"We no fight," lamented Circle Bear. He took a draw on the pipe and passed it to me.

It was less about fighting than having the will to live.

I was at a loss for advising Circle Bear on what he should do other than become a true leader and inspire his people to lift themselves from their apathy. The food supplies we'd brought might last a month or so. Then what? "The Miniconjou must learn ways of the White man."

Circle Bear gazed at me as though I'd committed some sort of blasphemy. He shook his head. "White man take. Kill buffalo. Take yellow metal. Give sickness." Anger lingered with its heavy presence upon the chief. "Women work, men fight, men hunt," he insisted. He was stubbornly committed to the old ways.

I recalled my pa telling me how the Jews at the time of Christ were stubborn about the Messiah and sharing with non-believers, whom they called gentiles. These Jews were referred to as stiff-necked. Well, Circle Bear seemed quite stiff-necked.

"Does Awentia hunt and fight?" asked Circle Bear.

I was initially taken aback, as I found the question inappropriate. It was none of his business. Then again, I figured it just might be a teaching moment. "Awentia has taken scalps, fought Cheyenne and Arapaho, and hunted elk. She is a good mother to our children, keeps house clean, honors Isa."

My response seemed to set the chief back a bit. He was quite obviously surprised. "You make arrows?"

"We both make arrows straight and true," I replied. "Awentia is a warrior woman."

Circle Bear was about to ask another question but paused as he cogitated on what I'd just said. Finally, he smiled. "Circle Bear need warrior women."

Well, that was progress. He was at least beginning to think about something besides sitting back and living on government handouts while his people wasted away.

"Miniconjou Lakota men must lead. Show women they are strong."

Circle Bear's eyes questioned me as to how this would be accomplished.

"To make Miniconjou strong, men work at Lakota ways and White man's ways. Help women, but hunt, fish, bring firewood, plant crops." I awaited the chief's response.

The idea of men helping the women was anathema to him. It simply wasn't done. "Miniconjou men break ponies, play games, race horses, fight enemy..." His voice trailed off. The men used to justify lying around and playing games by bringing in game to eat and fighting enemy tribes. He was now being confronted by a new life order. Occasionally stealing ponies, sleeping with one or more wives, and lying around in leisurely repose were no longer acceptable. Reality was beginning to sink in. He'd resisted it but knew that he'd have to accept the inevitable. What form that acceptance took was critically important to the survival of his people. "Isa wise," he said with a great sigh.

I'd been called a lot of things, both good and bad, but wise hadn't been one of them. The chief was nearly three times my age, yet wise enough to grasp the wisdom the young man before him had shared. I took time to think by taking a long pull on the pipe. I watched the smoke curl upward toward the vent at the top of the teepee. "McLaughlin no help. Circle Bear must show his people the way." It was essential that the chief step up to the task of leading.

"We feast tonight. *Wówanyanke!*" he declared with a broad smile. "Women eat too."

I figured that was his way of saying that the women would sit with the men to share the meal. We'd see.

* * *

Well, Circle Bear surprised me mostly. I say mostly, because there simply wasn't room in any single teepee for all the men and women to gather around to eat. There was also the matter of the children. We wound up with the chief hosting Morning Star and me, along with three of his warriors and their wives. One of the warriors had three wives, so that helped make for quite a gathering.

There was some discomfort at first, but the attendees became more relaxed as Circle Bear explained the new approach to life at the Standing Rock Agency. He puffed up some stories about me, including my hand-to-hand battle with the grizzly, and told his people that I had come as the great savior of the Miniconjou Lakota. I wanted to tell him about another savior but decided to share that at another time. For the present, I was being lifted up as a great warrior.

Through all of Circle Bear's talk, Morning Star suppressed the urge to break out laughing. She could barely eat between mirthful side glances at me.

For my part, I managed to keep a straight face. To laugh might have embarrassed our host. I distracted myself by thinking about how McLaughlin would handle the change in these people. Of course, that depended on Circle Bear continuing this new order he seemed to have bought into. We wouldn't know unless or until we came back to visit.

As I was reflecting on what might eventually become of these people, Circle Bear called out to me, "Will Isa stay with Miniconjou?"

I sure enough wished he'd asked me in private. "Isa and Awentia have home in Wyoming. We breed horses.

Miniconjou are strong, proud people. Circle Bear great leader. You learn new ways and have good life here."

Circle Bear was disappointed but wasn't about to let my response deter him from his revived sense of purpose. "Isa and Awentia come visit. See how great Miniconjou Lakota be."

I sure hoped he was right.

We figured to stay a couple of days to show the men how they could adapt to the new life. The couple of days turned into a week before we made the decision to head home.

Circle Bear was exceptionally grateful for the new positive actions that we'd injected into the daily lives of his people. Reluctant and unpracticed at first, the men surprised me by pitching in to help their wives. A couple of warriors even managed to bag a buck.

Moses made a couple of friends, so he was reluctant to have to bid them farewell. He was a bit hangdog as we departed. His feelings were mixed, however, as none of the children he'd met were riding horses yet. Riding his own horse had made him popular.

CHAPTER 19

HOMEWARD BOUND

Now, there were just the four of us heading home with three horses plus the packhorse. I'd given the other three packhorses to the Miniconjou with the hope that they'd use them to hunt rather than eat.

We camped the first night on a game trail between the Grand River and the tumbling waters of the Moreau. Given the rough terrain, I continued to be pleased with my decision to not bring a wagon. Game trails made for faster and likely safer travel, as we could more easily traverse ravines and narrow trails where a wagon could never pass.

After dinner, we sat as a family gazing up at the full moon and seemingly endless array of stars.

"I hear that the Crow think that a great spirit, a *Taa Narumi* or *Wi*." I mixed English with Comanche and Lakota to name the spirit god. That brought a smile to Morning Star's lips, as it noted our mixed family ancestry. "They say that when the moon is full, the great spirit sleeps. While the great spirit sleeps, the evil ones eat away at the moon until it is but a sliver in the night sky. The great spirit awakens and rebuilds the moon. Then the great spirit goes back to sleep, and the cycle is repeated. This is the way the Crow keep track of the months."

"What do Whites call this?" asked Morning Star.

"When the moon grows larger in the sky, it is called a waxing moon. When it becomes smaller, it is called a waning moon." I chuckled. "It seems easier than worrying about evil spirits. I think God probably prefers such a simpler version."

"Does Isa think Circle Bear will do as you urged him?" asked Morning Star, turning to a more serious subject.

"We can hope. He must lead his people in the White man's ways if they are to survive."

Moses looked unhappy. "Will boys and girls have food?" he asked. This was a very serious question for so young a boy.

"We hope and pray that they will, son," I replied. I knew that we couldn't be certain, as the Lakota reliance on the Standing Rock Agency wavered from bare subsistence to desperation. They must learn to fend for themselves.

* * *

Rain clouds greeted us the next morning as we ate breakfast. The sooner we returned to the trail, the better. I broke out the slickers from our packhorse in preparation for a possible storm.

The game trail was especially challenging as it took more twists and turns and presented switchbacks where the hillsides were steeper. I wasn't excited by the prospect of negotiating a rain-slicked path, especially for Moses in his modified saddle.

As we rode around a sharp bend and just as distant thunder could be heard, I spotted a rock overhang that would offer shelter from the storm. Taabe was first to the rock shelter and chased away some deer, though not before catching a fawn for his dinner.

I led our procession under the overhung just as rain-drops began to spatter on the rocky trail. With the combination of water and moss, the trail was quickly turning dangerously slippery. We were fortunate to have found shelter. We even set the slickers so that rain wouldn't splash us.

We thought we were safe until the sound of unshod hooves reached our ears. A place such as the one we were using to huddle from the storm would likely be known to most any Indians in the region. While the tribes had generally been at peace, we could never be certain. Just in case, I slipped the Marlin from its saddle scabbard and motioned to Morning Star to do the same. We checked our loads. Morning Star placed Michael at a far corner of our shelter and told Moses to watch over him.

Four soaked-to-the-skin Indians soon emerged from the bend in the trail and stood before us astride their war ponies. Their facial expressions were hard to read thanks to the rain.

Morning Star recognized them. "They Miniconjou Lakota," she whispered to me.

"*Hau, mitákuye oyás'e.*" I bade them *welcome* in the Lakota tongue. "Me Isa. This Awentia, daughter of Wapi-tiyu Okle." My words seemed to make no impression upon them. From the direction they had come, I assumed they were headed back to Standing Rock Agency. They would not in any case have been party to the recent goings on at Circle Bear's teepee. "Circle Bear *kola*," I added that their chief was my friend.

The four sat in silence, as rain dripped from their near-naked bodies. The lead warrior made an angry face and began to move toward us.

"*Wowahwa*." I raised my free hand and said *peace* in Lakota. It had no effect.

The warrior continued toward us as though ready to forcibly push us from the shelter.

I brought the muzzle of my rifle up and pointed it in the Lakota's general direction. "*Katá*," I warned.

At the word for *kill*, the warrior stopped. Through dark, angry eyes, he looked from me to Morning Star and back to me. He freed his warclub from his saddle. "*Sukawaka*," he growled. "*Katá wasichus*." An evilness darkened his face as he leered at Morning Star. "*Winyan*."

He was letting us know that he wanted our horses and would kill me, the White man, to get them. After such a peaceful meeting with Circle Bear, I lamented that this was quickly turning into what could become a tragic event.

The warrior's three companions moved their ponies to either side of the leader.

Without warning, Morning Star raised her rifle, aimed, and blasted the warclub from the warrior's hand, nicking his fingers badly.

The warrior's horse reared up, tossing him to the ground. The other Lakota were too shocked to react.

Morning Star swung her rifle toward the other three. "*Wiiyuka*," she seethed.

Struggling to turn on the slippery trail in the pouring rain, the horse of one of the warriors began to slide down the steep slope with his rider aboard, while the other two managed to disappear around the bend. Their leader, holding his bloodied hand, scurried off to join them.

I turned to Morning Star. "I hoped to make peace."

She shook her head. "They *wiiyuka*…cowards. No make peace." Regrettably, she was right. They were among the younger warriors who were unwilling to accept the decisions of their elders to give up the fight against the Whites and go to the reservations.

"I expect they'll be ashamed when they get back to Circle Bear's camp." The rain finally began to let up. We saw no more of the four Lakota but heard their angry words and noise as they apparently managed to recover and find another way around us. I hoped they'd in fact head to their encampment and not muster the courage to come after us. Whatever they decided, we'd remain mindful that others of similar intent might yet be encountered.

"What did those men want, Pa?" asked Moses as we gathered ourselves to get back on the trail.

"They were looking for something but decided to leave," I was sort of right.

"Why did Ma shoot?" He was full of questions. I suppose he was at the early stages of figuring out life.

"The man was not nice," said Morning Star before I could respond. "He is gone. We are going home." That was the end of the discussion. There'd be no more questions.

* * *

I was pleased to cross the Belle Fourche River the next day, as that put plenty of miles between us and the

Standing Rock Agency. It had felt satisfying to have brought them much-needed gifts, but I worried that Circle Bear's commitment to changing the ways of the Miniconjou Lakota might be short-lived. This would be especially so if he passed away with no strong leader to follow. I found myself worried that Morning Star might yearn to make a regular thing of transporting food and supplies to her people. That would be a fool's errand as they'd never learn to be self-sufficient.

"We never return," stated Morning Star with conviction as she rode close behind me. "They foolish." She seemed resigned to their fate. "Lose hope, lose life," she added. That further confirmed that she, too, doubted that they would continue to strive to learn the White man's ways and support themselves.

"Did you smell it?" I asked. I'd detected the faint aromas of alcohol in the Miniconjou camp.

She nodded.

We had found what some referred to as firewater stored in the Miniconjou camp. Liquor would surely continue the downward slide of her people if laziness and dependence weren't enough.

"Awentia spill bottles."

I smiled. They'd likely obtain more, though I admired her. Emptying the liquor bottles was a well-intended act and would spare the Miniconjou any drunkenness for a short time. I'd seen men of different races destroy themselves with the intoxicating spirits that altered minds. I wasn't against alcohol, but I detested what it could do to the senses, so I chose to drink very little and only ceremonially. Morning Star and I had discussed growing grapes on the ranch to make wine but decided against it for now.

While resupplying would have made some sense, we

decided to skirt around Deadwood and Rapid City. There was no point in pressing our luck, especially if we encountered that nasty trio in Rapid City. I had managed to bag an elk early on in our visit with Morning Star's people, so I had made plenty of jerky for our journey home. I reckoned we'd be well fed for the trail.

We made great progress over the next several days. Fording the Cheyenne River was a tad easier, especially without having to worry about three packhorses heavily loaded with gifts for the Miniconjou Lakota. It was also early July, and the river wasn't raging quite so much.

We soon found ourselves on the Cheyenne to Deadwood Trail. By my reckoning, we would arrive at a town named Hats Creek in a couple of days. As Captain Hayes had explained, Hats Creek had briefly been a military outpost set up by a Captain Egan out of the Fort Laramie garrison back in 1874. However, it was turned into a stagecoach station a couple of years later. Hayes told me that they regularly dealt with stagecoach robbers and hostile Indians, especially on the trail north to Deadwood.

Since the place was originally the product of protecting the miners during the rush for Black Hills gold, I held low expectations for Hats Creek. I surely expected no improvement over what we'd encountered in Rapid City. However, we did need to resupply, so we would visit the town. Regardless of the reasons behind the formation of a town on the frontier.

I found myself beginning to notice commonalities. For one thing, controversial concerns seemed to draw folks like moths to a lantern. Such concerns, like the weather, water sources, politics, Indian attacks, and more, become regular topics that either bring folks together or yank them apart. Most everyone seems to have an opinion about something, and the more that gather in a community, the more opinions flourish. As schools, stores, churches, and the law become part of the community, accountability is fostered. What many lose sight of is that since people are imperfect, so are their communities.

"What Isa think?" Morning Star had ridden up alongside me. With the wider trail, we could bunch up a bit.

I smiled. She sure enough knew me well. "I was thinking on the towns we visit. None are perfect."

"People full of selves," she observed. "Too much emotion when things go bad. Leads to evil." She was right.

With Moses within earshot, I measured my words. Everything for him was a learning experience, especially what his parents said and believed. "Many are lazy, seek riches without work. There are good people but tainted by their need for self-preservation and self-gratification." These were heavy words for Moses, but he didn't interrupt for explanation.

Morning Star nodded. "Fearful men destroy others; destroy themselves."

"A loving God is stronger than fear," I observed. "Men become like what they worship."

"Bad men do not know God?" piped up Moses. He'd understood our message.

"That's true, my son," I replied. I led us to the side of the trail as a bright red stagecoach came charging past. Naturally, we all waved. I could make out a woman among the passengers who otherwise appeared to be men headed to Deadwood for a fresh start. Perhaps the woman was doing the same.

"Push horses hard," observed Morning Star.

"Likely another stage station to the north. They'll get

fresh horses." I thought on that a second, then smiled. "They must outrun evil men."

* * *

We were in good spirits and better than hallway home. An hour after the stagecoach had passed, Hats Creek loomed ahead. We crossed Rock Creek and reined in at the station. The station was nestled in the pine-clad hills of Hat Creek Valley. The station was built of logs and planks and included a post office, telegraph office, stock and hay barn, bakery, grocery, brewery, and blacksmith shop. There were several horses in the adjoining corral, and someone was busy caring for them. From their excited, still-lathered condition, I suspected they'd been the ones recently swapped out to afford the stagecoach a fresh team.

I hailed the station keeper, "Howdy! Y'all have a spot for some weary travelers?"

He was a burly sort wearing a black vest and a shirt that might have been white at some time long past. Suspenders held up his pants over well-worn boots. His size was no surprise, given that he doubled as blacksmith, hostler, groom, and stager. He dropped the bucket of feed and gave us a long once-over. "Door's o'er yonder, pilgrim. You an' yer squaw an' chile be welcome to rest up. Grub's in the kitchen," he said with a friendly sort of grin.

"Thanks kindly," I replied. We dismounted and hitched our horses. We entered the station and found a couple of tables. Morning Star headed to the kitchen and ladled out some stew that was warming on the stove. About the time we'd sat to enjoy the meal, the station keeper ambled in.

He stood a moment and smiled friendly-like. "My name's John. You folks be travelin' far?"

I nodded. "I'm Isa O'Toole. We're heading home to the North Platte country. We raise horses about a day west of Fort Laramie."

"Stagecoach horses?" he asked reflexively. From what little I'd seen of him among the stage horses, he appeared to be a lover of the beasts. The stage companies were always on the lookout for new horses.

"Quarter Horses," I replied.

He looked a little disappointed, but smiled, nevertheless. "Yuh been to Standing Rock?"

I suspect our Indian attire was a clue to his observation. I took a generous spoonful of stew. "Your stew is right good." After a sip of coffee, I responded to his question. "My wife is Miniconjou. We visited her people."

"Sad," he said rather simply. "Ain't the proud people they once was."

"Government's no help," I noted.

"Shouldn't be needed. Injuns need to haul themselves up an' learn new ways. You be part Injun, ain't yuh?"

"My ma is Penateka Comanche," I replied.

The station keeper calmly poured himself a cup of coffee. "I fought with Rip Ford back in fifty-eight."

"My pa scouted for Captain Ford," I shared.

"Small world, ain't it," responded the station keeper.

Morning Star and Moses had pretty much devoured their bowls of stew, and Michael had been fed while I was chatting with John. I found myself caught up with where the conversation was headed.

The station keeper paused suddenly and ran to the window. "Road agents!" he hollered. He pointed to a gun rack along one wall. "Grab them guns," he directed.

By now, we'd heard the clatter of hooves as well.

Morning Star and I rushed to the gun rack and grabbed a couple of Winchester Model 1880 lever-action rifles along with handfuls of .38-56 caliber cartridges. They were effective killing machines in the hands of hunters or warriors. "You know them?" I asked.

"Been here a few months back. Nasty varmints." He replied. "Better git yer chillun back in the kitchen."

I hustled Moses and Michael to the kitchen at the rear of the station and told them to stay there and remain quiet no matter what. I returned to Morning Star's side at a window on the opposite side of the door from the station keeper. "Our horses!" I exclaimed. "We can't let them steal our horses!"

I saw Taabe standing among our horses, hackles up and raring for a fight.

"Not to worry. They be lookin' fer money," said John with some assurance. "If yuh got any in yer bags, they be after it." He saw Taabe. "Thet yer dog?"

"He's a wolf," I called to him.

"They'd as soon shoot the critter as look at him. If he be yers, yuh better call him in," he advised.

I dashed out and guided Taabe inside in the nick of time.

Five men came charging up to the station. They appeared to have been riding hard, as their horses were well lathered and nostrils flared with heavy breathing. I wondered whether they were running to something or from something. Regardless, they looked to be focused on us for the present. All of them wore one or two bandoliers and were brandishing rifles, mostly Spencer models from the look of them. "Git out here, John!" one of the men hollered.

The station keeper didn't budge.

"Got a posse chasin' us! We need fresh hosses!" the road agent leader demanded.

John swung his window open, poked his rifle through, and blew one of the road agents from his saddle. "Told yuh varmints tuh stay clear of here!" he yelled. He levered another round and winged a second man.

Now, the others brought their guns into the fray. They opened fire on the window where John no longer stood. Bullets plowed through the station window and into the back wall.

"Y'all can chip in any time," John said with a smile toward Morning Star and me.

I wasn't generally inclined to kill folks, and neither was Morning Star, but this battle was heating up, and I wasn't especially anxious for some random ricochet to reach the kitchen where our sons were hiding. This had become a matter of self-defense. Following John's lead, I swung open the window we were standing at and took a bead on the apparent leader of the road agents. My aim was a tad off as my bullet creased his skull and knocked him from his saddle.

Morning Star was in the process of aiming when a slew of riders galloped in. The road agents still in their saddles turned tail, urging their cayuses into as much gallop as the weary beasts could manage. Three of the newcomers reined in at the station while others pursued the escaping road agents.

"Well, that figgers!" exclaimed John. "They be late tuh the party!"

We followed John from the station.

"Howdy, John," said the leader of the posse. "Ain't seen you in some time. Much obliged that y'all helped us out."

The station keeper shook his head ruefully, then smiled. "Yer late," he stated flat out.

"You folks okay?" the posse leader asked.

By now, the dead man had been dragged over to a bench in front of the station, and the unconscious bandit leader was placed beside him.

"They tried to rob the Weston's little store south of here, but we were waiting for them."

"What do y'all figure to do with them?" I asked.

John looked over at me and rolled his eyes.

"See yonder tree?" asked the posse leader. "Well, we got plenty of rope."

Part of my—actually, all of me—wanted to stop a lawless lynching, but we were in no position to prevent it. Then, an idea came to me. "We have a couple of young children with us. Do y'all mind doing your justice somewhere else?" If we couldn't stop a hanging, at least we might not have to witness it.

John looked at me as though I was asking for the moon and stars.

The posse leader had been gathering coils of rope, but my plea had gotten his attention. He looked to be reconsidering. Finally, he gave us a long, hard look. "Yuh got a point. When the men get back here with the others, we'll mosey over yonder out of sight and take care of what needs taking care of."

John was amazed.

"Thanks kindly," I said with heartfelt gratitude, but a lingering sadness that the justice was being corrupted. It did little to assuage my feelings that the bandits had done something worthy of the ultimate punishment. I thought about what my pa told me of the words of Jesus at the well when he forgave the woman but told her to go and sin no more. Apparently, these road agents had been habitual sinners and would finally meet their fate. I had to remind myself that there were no courts of law handy around these parts, and the men of the posse likely would have served as jury had there been a courtroom.

Helpless to do more, I headed back inside to bury my feelings in a cup of coffee and a piece of apple pie I'd seen in the kitchen.

Morning Star followed me in. "You do good," she assured me and reinforced it with a hug and kiss. "Boys, come out now," she called.

We had no intention of witnessing the executions, so we decided to leave after I finished that delicious slice of apple pie.

Apparently, John held no interest either. He was busying himself with shoeing a horse as we departed. He did pause to wave goodbye and quickly went back to his work.

* * *

Our brief visit to Hats Creek had been memorable to say the very least. It wasn't every day that folks got to do battle with lawless desperados on the run. Call them bandits or road agents or what you will, they posed a serious threat. Many a stagecoach had been victimized by the particular bunch that we'd faced.

After the Hats Creek experience, we decided to take an overland route roughly parallel to that road. We didn't feature the possibility of being waylaid by more road agents. I reckoned to let the stage line and any posses worry about those threats.

We made great progress over the next six days, finally reaching the north bank of the North Platte River with no further threats to life and limb. Michael seemed to thoroughly enjoy his position behind Morning Star's saddle, and Moses had become an expert rider. We stopped often to rest and water the horses, and I managed to kill a deer that kept us fed. It was now simply a matter of crossing the river and picking up the Oregon Trail and heading home.

CHAPTER 20

THE RANCH

Anxious to be back at the Laramie Cross Breed Ranch, we bypassed the Freeman spread. While it was always enjoyable to visit George and Running Waters, we were fixated on resuming life at home. As we approached our ranch, I was struck by how established it appeared. It was no longer some early-stage venture, but a mature operating endeavor.

As we turned southward from the river, we caught sight of Cutter in the distance wrangling some beeves on his spread. Ahead of us, Donovan and Moon were leading a couple of two-year-old Quarter Horses from the east pasture. They waved their hats and came riding toward us.

"Welcome home," called Donovan, as they neared.

We all reined in. Smiles abounded.

"Y'all look like you've never been on the trail. Must be livin' right," noted Moon.

It must have been the elixir of joy at being home that made it appear that we weren't trail-weary. "We're happy to be home," I rejoined.

"Well, y'all hustle on to yer home. It's gettin' late in the day, an' Pearl oughta be fixin' up some rib-stickin' grub," said Donovan. "I'll get Moon here to go invite Cutter and Esmeralda."

Morning Star and I looked at each other. It sure felt right fine to be back home. "Mighty obliged, Chester. See you in a bit." The two hands rode off, and we nudged our trail-weary cayuses on up the path to home.

It didn't take long to take care of the horses and unpack. We'd just about run out of our food supplies.

Pearl's cooking would be a welcome relief. Despite being tired, the camaraderie of our ranching family would be uplifting. We raced to freshen up a bit before everyone arrived. We had the biggest table, so it made sense for everyone to gather around in our kitchen.

Soon enough, Pearl arrived with a baby under one arm, Donovan in tow, and carrying enough food to feed an army.

We recounted our travel experiences, including concerns over the deplorable situation at the Standing Rock Agency. The tales of the ne'er do-wells in Rapid City, the Lakota warriors we met during the rainstorm, and the battle with road agents especially caught the fancy of Cutter and Moon. I guess they were starved for excitement.

We conversed animatedly until we couldn't put another morsel in our bulging bellies. Trail weariness began to take effect, and our guests were observant enough to catch on. We needed peace and rest in our very own beds. As we began post-meal cleanup, Donovan cleared his throat. "One more thing, Isa," he said. He handed me an envelope. Printed above my name was the logotype and address of the Cheyenne Club. I sighed. "Thanks, Chester." I set it on the table. It could wait until morning.

* * *

My, but it was absolutely delightful to once again spend a night in our home. While Morning Star and I loved the outdoors and sleeping under the stars, there was a part of us that had grown comfortable with ranch life and the aromas and general feeling of our very own home. Frankly, it wasn't unlike what our Indian ancestors likely felt at the familiarity of their wickiups, hovels, lodges, and teepees. Morning Star could vividly recall growing up in her parents' teepee up near the Laramie Range at the headwaters of the North Platte, just as I had fond memories of my folks' house at the Rising Cross Ranch. Whether aromas of cooking or fresh-churned butter or tanning hides, the home was a treasure for our memories.

Come crack of dawn, I sat at the edge of our bed, yawned, and stretched before putting on my pants and yanking on my boots. Morning Star was asleep beside me. I was getting my arms into the sleeves of my shirt as I walked into the kitchen to the smell of fresh-brewed coffee. Morning Star had been up early, made the coffee, and gone back to bed. The unopened envelope on the table beckoned.

I eyeballed it for a moment but walked over and poured myself a cup of coffee. Finally, I took a seat at the kitchen table and picked up the envelope. I hefted it for a moment, put it back down, and sipped my coffee. With a sigh, I unsheathed my knife and slit open the envelope. I pulled out a letter and a pamphlet of some sort. Taking another slow sip of coffee, I unfolded the letter and began to read.

> *Dear Mr. O'Toole,*
>
> *It is my pleasure to inform you that the Cheyenne Club has voted to invite you to*
>
> *become a member.*
>
> *Enclosed is a pamphlet describing the nature and rules of our organization. Our entrance fee is $100, and annual dues are $30.*
>
> *Please RSVP your acceptance of our invitation by the 30th of August 1882 with accompanying remittance.*
>
> *Sincerely,*
>
> *Arthur Teschemacher*

Well, I wasn't surprised. I'd rather expected this and admit to being a tad flattered. I reckoned that I was the first and only invitee who wasn't fully White-skinned. I stared at the letter and reread it.

About this time, I heard Morning Star's footsteps padding into the kitchen and over to the coffee. She poured herself a cup and sat beside me.

I nudged the letter toward her, so it was easier for her to read. "What do you think?"

"Isa expect this," she said definitively. "We have decision to make."

"The money is no bother," I reflected. "I'll bet they would never invite George."

"Because he Black?" she asked.

"The members that run the club are prominent folks from east coast, as well as gentlemen ranchers from British and European families. It's rather exclusive. They wouldn't invite me but for the influence of a big cattleman like Charles Goodnight."

"And?" Morning Star pressed.

"It's not a fit for us and the Laramie Cross Breed Ranch. We're not pretentious folk here. I hope they won't be so offended that they won't buy my Quarter Horses, but I figure to turn them down."

Morning Star smiled. She'd known all along what my answer would be. "I think they invite Isa as a courtesy."

I chewed on that hard truth for a moment and sipped more coffee. "I guess I shouldn't be anyone's token half-breed," I joked with a laugh.

"Isa hungry?" she urged.

"Hungry for Awentia," I smothered her with kisses, then let her squirm away from my embrace to cook up our first breakfast at home after our long journey to Standing Rock Agency.

* * *

It was mid-July, and our two-year-olds needed to be driven to prospective buyers in Cheyenne. I was already thinking of another trip to Texas, though the entire family would come along on this one. I reckoned one more winter here in Wyoming before heading southward.

Leaving the house, I met up with Donovan at the corral. "You ready for us to drive them to Cheyenne, Chester?"

He nodded. "Should be ready in about two weeks. We have a couple of spirited horses that are taking a bit longer to saddle break."

I chuckled. "Let me guess. Sired by Mukue."

"True that," he responded with a knowing laugh.

"How many Quarter Horses are ready?" I knew the number but asked anyway. Guess I was asserting myself a bit.

"Nineteen, Isa. I hope that bank down there can handle all that money." He guffawed at his own humor.

"What do you think of expanding our market and shipping horses to Texas by rail?"

He pondered that a moment. "I expect the cayuses would be up to it. You of a mind to do it soon?"

"Next year for sure. I know Charles Goodnight at the JA ranch was impressed, and I'm sure there are ranchers down in Bandera that crave our stock. I figure to send some inquiry letters to some Texas folks."

"What about your ranch near Bandera?" asked Donovan.

"I reckon to bring the family down there and spend a year or so. You've got a handle on everything here."

He nodded. He flashed me a look that said he suspected that I might stay in Texas permanently.

"With the railroads these days, I reckon to spend winters down in Texas and summers up here."

"Why not head there this fall?" he suggested.

I hadn't really considered making the move so soon. "Might not be a bad idea, Chester. I'll have to talk it over with Awentia." With that, I climbed over the corral fence. I held my hand out toward one of those extra-spirited two-year-olds. He glared at me suspiciously, but his curiosity was having its way with him. With a snort and bob of his head, he came trotting over to investigate the white lump in the palm of my hand. I didn't move a muscle as he edged closer. The stallion gave a final bob of his great head and snatched the sugar from my hand. Mission completed, he dashed back to the far side of the corral. Little wonder that patience was a huge factor in dealing with horses. They were like humans in that trust was critically important.

I had found that hope breathed eternal in those who sought purpose in life, triumphing over the poor souls who strove not and inexorably awaited their fate.

CHAPTER 21

CHEYENNE EVILS

Donovan, Moon, and I drove eighteen saddle-broke two-year-old Quarter Horses to Cheyenne. Cutter stayed back at the ranches as much to enjoy his wedded bliss as help ensure that chores were tended to and the place was secure. The journey was uneventful other than spotting the usual herds of elk, buffalo, and deer. We sighted occasional grizzly and even a mountain lion, but they stayed clear of us and our herd.

All eighteen Quarter Horses were sold to ranchers in Cheyenne. Amazingly, no one made any reference to my heritage, and I felt a sense of admiration over the quality of the horses we offered for sale. When they'd all been sold, we had to make promises to those who missed out that we'd be back next year. Word was getting out that the Laramie Cross Breed Ranch was delivering the best Quarter Horses to be had west of the Mississippi.

We deposited the sale proceeds in the bank, as it made no sense to be carrying cash around. Donovan even opened an account for him and Pearl.

We didn't reckon to hang around Cheyenne for long.

However, I made a point to visit the Cheyenne Club. The gentlemen at the club displayed no ill feelings at my turning down their kind membership invitation. I actually felt a sense of relief from them.

Arthur Teschemacher even offered a thousand dollars for Mukue. I was flattered but naturally turned him down. He was a nice enough fellow, but I had a sense that trouble lay ahead, as these wealthy gentleman ranchers sought ever greater control over Wyoming ranching and control's bedfellow: power. While I wasn't joining the Cheyenne Club, I reckoned to sign up with the Wyoming Stock Growers Association. I figured it to be a way to keep an eye on the goings on throughout Wyoming.

With our business in Cheyenne completed, we enjoyed a fine dinner and made plans to head home the next morning.

Other than a couple of inebriated cowboys casting some racial slurs our way as they staggered by, the evening went pleasantly.

* * *

A crystal-clear day in Wyoming was so common as to be considered the norm. Winter storms were quickly forgotten as we enjoyed the warmth of the July sun. We headed northward at a leisurely pace, as there was no point in unnecessarily pushing our horses. The trail was easy, as we followed the Cheyenne-Deadwood stage road. I'd estimate we were about two hours into our journey when we heard horses galloping behind us.

"Who could be in such an all-fired hurry?" I asked Donovan as he rode alongside me.

Donovan shrugged, then looked behind us. "Isa!

There's a bunch of them, and they're riding hard. Waving rifles."

Moon and I looked back. Donovan was right. Worse, there looked to be at least seven, and they looked like they were fixing to bring us trouble for whatever reason suited them. The first true hint of that was when one of them fired at us.

Waiting wasn't an option. Some cottonwoods stood off to our right, and we bolted for them. We quickly found a natural indentation between two trees that was defensible. We yanked our rifles from their scabbards and picketed out horses. By the time we'd nestled defensively into that depression between the two trees, the riders were just about upon us.

They arrived at the spot where we'd left the road, and one of them pointed to the spot where we'd settled in. He yelled something, and they all charged toward us with guns blazing.

"Don't kill the Injun," one of them shouted.

This was personal. These men had burrs in their saddles over Indians. Bullets were buzzing past hot and heavy, so we kept our heads low until they got close enough to make our return more fire effective.

They were roughly a hundred feet from us and coming on hard when, at my signal, we finally poked our heads up and returned fire. At least two were blown from their saddles, but out of the corner of my eye, I saw poor Joe Moon catch a bullet in his face. He collapsed and quickly breathed his last.

The attackers veered off to gather for another charge.

It gave Donovan and me time to reload.

"How's Moon?" I asked.

Donovan confirmed what I'd feared. "He's gone, Isa."

I realized that Donovan had caught a round in the

arm, but it wasn't mortal. Thus far, I was unscathed. "You okay?" I asked.

Donovan nodded.

There were now five of them against us two.

Donovan reached over and placed Moon's rifle between us. It afforded us a little more firepower.

"Here they come!" I exclaimed as the attackers rallied for a second charge.

They came on hell bent for leather, pouring as much lead at us as they could muster.

We returned fire, but it looked as though they intended to overrun us. I took down a horse, and Donovan shot another from the saddle. Then, Donovan took a bullet in his ribs and fell back, struggling to catch air. This was not going well.

They were upon us! A horse bowled me over as two attackers launched themselves on top of me. Another man stood over Donovan and put another bullet into him. He lay still.

Struggle as I might, I found myself smothered by the attackers. I was rendered helpless, as my arms were bound behind my back.

"You be ours now, Injun," said one of the men. His laugh was as evil as could be imagined.

I recognized him as one of the drunks who'd passed by us the night before. I mustered enough voice to cry out, "What do you…"

Epilogue

The American western frontier was mostly unforgiving, a meeting of savagery and civilization. More and more towns were springing up, and they served as bellwethers to the civilizing of the frontier. *Wyoming Destiny: Hope Triumphs Over Fate* offers a peek into the courage, faith, endurance, and pure grit entailed in the conquest of the west. I decided at age fifteen that it was time to venture out on my own. Little did I know that the Great Plains Indian Wars loomed ahead. I'm twenty-two now with a warrior woman wife, two children, and a Quarter Horse breeding ranch in Wyoming. The world around me was a mix of the majestic natural beauty of a rugged landscape and lurking dangers. This environment seemed to attract the best and worst of humans.

The frontier? Exactly what is the frontier? I reckon it to be the untamed boundary between the known and unknown, the majestic and sublime. It is a space of vast landscapes fostering inspiration, opportunity, and purpose. It is a metaphor of life, challenging the traveler to navigate its soul and embrace its very unfamiliarity.

Life expectancy on the frontier was nothing like today. A male Indian did well to live beyond age thirty, and women could expect to live a tad less. Little wonder that older tribesmen were highly respected. Life expectancy for Whites wasn't much better. A White man on the frontier tended not to live beyond his late thirties. Notably, the brevity of life generally meant that folks had to mature sooner. By the time a man or woman reached age fifteen or sixteen, he or she was pretty much an adult in terms of others expecting him or her to carry an adult set of responsibilities.

Indians? I am half Comanche. While I've dealt with Kiowa, Arapaho, Crow, Cheyenne, Shoshone, and Ute, most of my experience has been with the Comanche and Lakota peoples. Dangers? Anthropology-minded folks claim there were as many as thirteen distinct tribes of Comanche, from the Quahadi or "antelope eaters" in the north to the Penateka or "honey eaters" in the south. Mix in Kiowa, Apache, and Tonkawa, and settlers had their hands full. The very name Comanche loosely translates in the Ute tribal language as *kumantsi* or "enemy."

Capture by the Comanche invariably led to terrible outcomes. A fearsome lot those tribes were. The horse, coupled with a long history of trade for the latest weapons and farm-grown foods in and around the Comancheria, produced a highly aggressive nomadic culture heavily dependent on the buffalo and slave trade. For example, Penateka Comanche Chief Buffalo Hump led more than 600 warriors on a raid through the heart of Texas in August 1840, murdering Texans, looting the city of Victoria, and looting and burning Linnville on their march to the Gulf of Mexico. It was not until 1858 that Texas Ranger John Salmon "Rip" Ford led a force of 102 heavily armed Texas Rangers and 100 Indian allies that brought the Comanche to their knees at the Battle of Little Robe Creek on the Canadian River in Oklahoma, as described in my pa's Frontier Chronicle *Warpath: Jack's Faith is Tested.*

The northwestern plains were peopled by many tribes, but especially the Sioux, comprised of three groups: Dakota, Nakota, and Lakota. The Lakota were made up of seven subgroups: Oglalas (famed for Red Cloud and Crazy Horse), Hunkpapas (famed for Sitting Bull), Miniconjous (People Who Live Near Water), Oohenunpas (Two Kettles), Itazipacolas (No Bows), Brulés (Burnt Thighs), and Sihásapas (Blackfeet). The Lakota history was no less combative than Comanche, Crow, or Cheyenne. Despite the violence of the frontier, it's notable that the Lakota held to a worthy set of virtues, especially generosity, courage, fortitude, and wisdom. The North Platte country referred to in *Wyoming Destiny: Hope Triumphs Over Fate* was part of the Wyoming Territory established in 1868. The Dakota Territory bordered it to the east.

The wolf plays an important role in Wolf's Tales, both in terms of my Comanche name, Isa, translating to wolf, and to my furry wolf companion, Taabe. There are many misconceptions about wolves. The Indians venerated them for their loyalty, power, courage, ferocity, sagacity, and devotion to family. I am sensitive to ranchers viewing wolves as a scourge that kills their cattle and to hunters who seek the elk, buffalo, deer, and moose upon which wolves prefer to prey. I certainly don't want wolves killing my livestock. The wolf is nevertheless part of the struggle between predator and prey. It could be said that life and death in the wild are part of its wonder. God gave each animal its allotted lifespan. How far does mankind go in tipping the balance one way or another?

There were plenty of wild animals on the frontier. I do refer to bison as buffalo. Just for the record, bison and buffalo are quite different. Visualize the water buffalo and then the shaggy, awkward bulk of the American bison. Seems that "buffalo" came into common usage in America to refer to the bison, so I've chosen to use buffalo in my writings. Notable too is that the evasive four-legged critter many unwary folks refer to as an antelope is properly called a pronghorn. Catch one if you can. There is also a big predatory cat that most folks in North America call a mountain lion, but also answers to puma, cougar, or panther.

Historically notable in the Wolf's Tales is that the longest and most used cattle trail was the Great Western Trail from 1874 to 1893. It ran from Matamoros, Mexico, to Val Marie, Canada. As many as three hundred thousand cattle each year would eventually be driven up that Great Western Trail, especially by the likes of famed rancher Charles Goodnight.

I enjoyed no modern creature comforts. Invention and popularization of telephones were decades into the future. Transportation? Horses, mules, and oxen—ridden or pulling wagons—were the vehicles of choice. I enjoyed no refrigerator to preserve sweet treats. There were no flush toilets or showers. Folks mostly ate what grazed upon or grew from the land. Learning was squeezed from the few books that might be found, especially the Holy Bible. Can't say as the living of the era was luxurious unless you counted the sheer grandeur of majestic landscapes and of nights so quiet you could hear the stars twinkling.

To fully appreciate the place, you simply had to love the incredible beauty of the outdoors. Fishing the meandering Guadalupe River in Texas or the chill waters of

Wyoming's North Platte and Laramie Rivers, taking in the grandeur of Yellowstone National Park, hunting deer and pronghorn, raising cattle and horses, and reaping the bounteous yield of the rich soil was sheer joy for a courageous visionary few. For a teen on the frontier, life could be pretty good…mostly. Otherwise, it was downright dangerous.

Thus far, I was quickly growing to manhood. My vision quest had led me on a path known only to God. I was striving to conquer personal fears and prejudices, fight Indians and bandits, defend against wild beasts, travel the wild country, and drive cattle and horses. With it, I found the love of my life and a life purpose. As you have seen, I especially draw upon my faith and what I was taught by my parents. And yet, all of this is constantly tested. I had to learn to trust in instincts forged from my biblical and life lessons. Yes, I'm on a frontier adventure and more. And you, dear reader, will now be able to follow me, Isa O'Toole, as I seek my own way in life and share my adventures. May God ever bless me and Morning Star.

Glossary

DEFINITIONS

Bear sign—Cowboy slang for donuts.

Big Father or Great Father—All-powerful Indian deity.

Bota bag—A canteen fashioned from leather and popular among Indians, mountain men, and many travelers of the western frontier.

Cold Camp—Camp without a campfire, generally done to avoid the smoke that might alert threats.

Dog run—The sheltered space or breezeway between two sections of some southern ranch houses. Living quarters were usually on one side and sleeping quarters on the other.

Fletch—The fin-shaped bird feathers on an arrow that help stabilize its flight.

Gallery—A synonym for porch. Folks in the west often called the structures across the front of their homes galleries.

Life debt—A cultural phenomenon in which

someone whose life is saved or spared by another becomes indebted or in some way connected to their savior.

Pemmican—Lean dried strips of meat pounded into a paste, mixed with fat and berries, and then pressed into small cakes.

Possibles bag (aka parfleche)—A leather or canvas sack carried by cowboys and containing essentials like soap, matches, bandages, extra spurs, smoke makings, and playing cards

Remuda—A herd of horses frequently deployed on trail drives and by Plains Indians.

Rendezvous—Annual celebratory gathering of mountain men.

Sand—Courage.

Shaman—Medicine man.

Teepee—An enclosed conical transportable shelter constructed of long poles and buffalo hides with a vent at the top to permit smoke to escape.

Travois—A wedge-shaped structure constructed of two poles and a cross-beam lashed together and dragged behind horses, mules, or dogs by Plains Indians.

Wahg!—Mountain man version of hail the camp or hello.

COMANCHE TRANSLATIONS

Aitu—Not good

Ana o'a hi'it—Phrase for "desire to eat"

Ap—Father

Aruka—Deer

Eetu—Bow

Ekakwitsubaitu—Lightning

Ekapitu—Red

Eekasahpana paraiboo—Army officer (soldier chief)
Haa—Yes
Hawokatu—Hollow, loose
Hoikwa—Hunt, look for prey
Isa—Wolf
Isa wasu—Poison
Kaahaniitu—deceive, cheat
Kahni—Life
Kamakuna—Loved one
Kee—No
Kobe—Wild horse
Kohto—Build a fire
Kooitu—Die
Kuha—Hello
Kuhmabai—Married
Kuisa—Coyote
Kuuna—Fire
Kuya akatu—Afraid of
Kwakuru—Defeat someone
Kwihnai—Eagle
Mua—Moon
Mukue—Spirit
Nahuu—Knife
Natsuitu—Strong
NiyáŋkA—We eat
Numu—Cow, Cattle
Numunahkahnis—Family
Numunuu—Referring to the members of the Comanche tribes. Literally: people.
Ohapitu—Yellow
Onaa—Son or daughter
Paa—Water
Pabi—Friend
Paaka—Arrow

Peeka—Kill

Pia—Mother

Pia huutsuu—Bald eagle

Pia wa'óo—Comanche words for mountain lion, puma, or cougar.

Pihi—Heart

Pohya (or poya)—Walk

Puuka—Horse

Sunipu—Medicine (as in strong medicine)

Suumaru—Ten

Taa Narumi—Master; God

Taabe—Sun

Tabu—Coward

Tamu—Rabbit

Tasiwoo—Buffalo

Tenahpu—Man

Tomoobi—Sky

Tosa—White man or woman

Tosaabitu—White

Totsiyaa—Flower

Tumah tuyai—After life

Tuhibitu—Black

Tumhyokenu—Believe, trust

Tu Taiboo—Black man

Umaru—Rain

Unha haksi nahniaka—Phrase for "what's your name?"

Wa'ipu—Woman

Wasápe—Bear

Wutsutsuki—Rattlesnake

LAKOTA TRANSLATIONS

Akicita—Warrior
  Ate—Father
  Ayústan—Abandon, retreat, leave
  Enákiya—Stop
  Hau, mitákuye oyás'e—Welcome
  Igmuwatogla—Mountain lion
  Ínyan—Fire
  Isan—Knife
  Iya Tate—Wind
  Iyaya—Go, leave
  Jiji—Light hair
  Katá—Kill
  Kola—Friend (male)
  Kize—Fight
  Kte—Dead
  Maka—The earth and grandmother of all things
  Mas'óphiye—Trade or barter
  Mato—Bear, also eat
  Mini—Water
  Nagi—The spirit that has never been a man
  Nanji—Jealous
  Niya—Ghost
  Okin—Pretty
  Oyate—The people or nation
  Sapa—Black
  Ska—White
  Scan—Sky
  Sukawaka—Horse
  Sunkmanitu tanka—Wolf
  Takuwe—Why
  Tanka—Wolf

Tatanka—The great beast (patron of health, ceremonies, provision)

Unk—Created by Maka; embodies all evil beings

Unktehi—One who kills

Wakan Tanka—God (monotheistic)

Wamaka nagi—Animal spirit

Wanbli—Eagle

Wani—Four winds (weather)

Wasake—Strong

Wash tay—Good

Wasichus—White man

Wasna—Pemmican

Wi—The sun (chief of all gods)

Wica—Complete man

Wicasa—Man (gender)

Wicasa wakan—Shaman

Wiiya—Danger

WiiyakA—Marry

Wiiyuka—Coward

Wiiyukta—Love

Winyan—Woman

Wówaŋyaŋke—We eat

Wowahwa—Peace

Zuzeca—Snake

THANK YOU

Thank you for taking the time to read *Wyoming Destiny: Hope Triumphs Over Fate.* If you enjoyed it, please consider telling your friends or posting a short review. Word of mouth is an author's best friend and much appreciated.

Thank you.
Mark Greathouse

Acknowledgments

Authoring books doesn't simply happen in a vacuum. The author provides the creative talent and crafts the stories, but there's so much more that demands acknowledgment. There are lots of folks and places that contribute to my authoring endeavors. So it is with *Wyoming Destiny: Hope Triumphs Over Fate.* The tale is set in 1881 and transitions into 1882, sharing the trials and tribulations of a young man forced to meet the challenges inherent in the dangerous vastness of the western frontier. But this novel stands apart. At its core, it is also about the taming of that frontier. The protagonist epitomizes the freedom of America's western frontier and represents a final bastion of honor in America. The Wolf's Tales tale follows Jack O'Toole's earlier Frontier Chronicles series, beginning with his adventures in *Perilous Trails: Jack's Adventure Begins.* Hopefully, readers will find this fourth book in the Wolf's Tales series worthy of their time and emotional involvement. Saddle up and ride into the future with Isa O'Toole.

I've been blessed with many friends and family who have supported my writings. My wife Carolyn's reviews and encouragement were a huge help, along with very important tech support from our sons Mike and Matt. Thanks to my pastor Randy for his faith insights. Many more friends and family have contributed support at some level to the creation and publication of my Wolf's Tales, be it encouragement or advice.

Naturally, I am major grateful to the great folks at the Wise Wolf Books imprint of Wolfpack Publishing. The team they bring to publishing is first-rate in editing, cover design, and the myriad tasks that lead to successful book sales.

It's only right to acknowledge my ancestors. They were actual settlers of the South Texas frontier. In addition to inspiring me, they provided a quite helpful true-to-life framework as to the life and times on the Texas Nueces Strip. I've also personally walked the very landscapes traversed by my fictional and historical characters.

Most of my authoring has occurred in my office as decorated to channel my inner Texan, but my creative juices have often been inspired and my imagination stoked in cafés and coffee houses across America. My favorites were Hester's Café & Coffee Bar in Corpus Christi, TX; Nueces Café in Robstown, TX; Java Ranch Espresso Bar & Café in Fredericksburg, TX; PAX Coffee & Goods in Kerrville, TX; Ragged Edge Coffee House and Bantam Coffee Roasters in Gettysburg, PA; 1889 Coffee House in Helena, MT; Wild Joe's Coffee Shop, Bozeman, MT; Tumbleweed Café, Gardiner, MT; Dunn Brothers Coffee in Rapid City, SD; Postmasters Coffee & Bakery and Brio Coffeehouse in Waynesboro, PA; Birdie's Café and American Ice Co Café in Westminster, MD; Deja Brew Coffee House, New Oxford and Deja Brew at Miney Branch, Carroll Valley, PA; Baltimore Coffee & Tea Co., Frederick Coffee Company & Café, and Dublin Roasters in Frederick, MD; Qualle Café and Grounded Coffee & Bakery, Cherokee, NC; Palace Café, Amarillo, TX; and Unto Others Café, Lamar, CO. I must admit to also frequenting a few Dunkin Donuts and Starbucks around our fine nation. The décors and easy-listening music in these fine establishments combined with savory cups of coffee tended to set me in the right creative frame of mind. They also afforded engagement with many fine citizens of our nation.

Last but not least, I'm especially thankful for the many folks who have read and enjoyed my books.

I do believe it's important to acknowledge how the old west represents the brave pioneering spirit of settlers who met the challenges and transcended mere survival to enable America to achieve exceptional growth. The settling of the American frontier west is replete with tales of leveraging freedom for individual achievement. I hope you'll agree that reliving our past—even through history-based fiction—often has the effect of pointing the way to an ever-brighter future. Might we be up to it? I hope that the inspiration I've drawn from my having walked the very earth my characters have trodden, coupled with my extensive historical research, will enable readers to fully experience the grit, adventure, and passion of my characters while sensing aromas of gunsmoke, trail dust, leather, and bluebonnets.

Thanks kindly to all of you, and I hope you enjoyed *Wyoming Destiny: Hope Triumphs Over Fate.*

About the Author

Award-winning author Mark Greathouse's love for the western genre draws upon his deep family roots and love of the outdoors honed from teen years hiking the Appalachian Trail and family travels across America's frontier. Greathouse began writing full time after a successful career as a business executive and later as an entrepreneurial investor and advisor. His service as president of several business and community nonprofits led to their extraordinary growth. He holds a BA in English and MBA in marketing. Greathouse donates time and books annually to support wounded military warriors.

A member of Western Writers of America and the Wild West History Association, he also contributes articles on the history of America's west to western-themed magazines. Greathouse was recognized as a 2024 Finalist in western genre by the American Literary Book Awards for his sixth Tumbleweed Saga, *Nueces Truth: Texans Face War's Realities.*

www.ingramcontent.com/pod-product-compliance
Lightning Source LLC
Chambersburg PA
CBHW030908060726

47591CB00005B/1457